"But tell me, dear," Miss Marple said to Mrs. Dane Calthrop, "what do the village people—I mean the townspeople—say? Who do they think is responsible for the deaths?"

"Mrs. Cleat still, I suppose," said Joanna.

"Oh, no," said Mrs. Dane Calthrop. "Not *now*."

Miss Marple asked who Mrs. Cleat was. Joanna said she was the village witch.

Miss Marple finally said:

"Oh! But the girl was killed with a skewer, so I hear. Well, naturally that takes all suspicion away from Mrs. Cleat. Because, you see, she could ill-wish her, so that the girl would waste away and die of natural causes."

"Strange how those old beliefs linger . . ." said the Vicar.

"It isn't superstition we've got to deal with here, but facts . . ."

AGATHA CHRISTIE

THE MOVING FINGER

BERKLEY BOOKS, NEW YORK

This Berkley book contains the complete text
of the original hardcover edition. It has been
completely reset in a typeface designed for easy
reading, and was printed from new film.

THE MOVING FINGER

A Berkley Book / published by arrangement with
Dodd, Mead & Company

PRINTING HISTORY
Dodd, Mead edition published 1942
Dell edition / March 1979
Berkley edition / June 1984

ISBN: 0–425–06787–4

A BERKLEY BOOK TM® 757,375
Berkley Books are published by The Berkley Publishing Group,
200 Madison Avenue, New York, New York 10016.
The name ''BERKLEY'' and the stylized ''B'' with design
are trademarks belonging to Berkley Publishing Corporation.

PRINTED IN THE UNITED STATES OF AMERICA

I

I have often recalled the morning when the first of the anonymous letters came.

It arrived at breakfast and I turned it over in the idle way one does when time goes slowly and every event must be spun out to its full extent. It was, I saw, a local letter with a typewritten address. I opened it before the two with London postmarks, since one of them was clearly a bill, and on the other I recognized the handwriting of one of my more tiresome cousins.

It seems odd, now, to remember that Joanna and I were more amused by the letter than anything else. We hadn't, then, the faintest inkling of what was to come—the trail of blood and violence and suspicion and fear.

One simply didn't associate that sort of thing with Lymstock.

I see that I have begun badly. I haven't explained Lymstock.

1

When I took a bad crash flying, I was afraid for a long time, in spite of soothing words from doctors and nurses, that I was going to be condemned to lie on my back all my life. Then at last they took me out of the plaster and I learned cautiously to use my limbs, and finally Marcus Kent, my doctor, clapped me on my back and told me that everything was going to be all right, but that I'd got to go and live in the country and lead the life of a vegetable for at least six months.

"Go to some part of the world where you haven't any friends. Get right away from things. Take an interest in local politics, get excited about village gossip, absorb all the local scandal. Small beer—that's the prescription for you. Absolute rest and quiet."

Rest and quiet! It seems funny to think of that now.

And so Lymstock—and Little Furze.

Lymstock had been a place of importance at the time of the Norman Conquest. In the twentieth century it was a place of no importance whatsoever. It was three miles from a main road—a little provincial market town with a sweep of moorland rising above it. Little Furze was situated on the road leading up to the moors. It was a prim, low, white house with a sloping Victorian veranda painted a faded green.

My sister Joanna, as soon as she saw it, decided that it was the ideal spot for a convalescent. Its owner matched the house, a charming little old lady, quite incredibly Victorian, who explained to Joanna that she would never have dreamed of letting her house if "things had not been so different nowadays—this terrible taxation."

So everything was settled, and the agreement signed, and in due course Joanna and I arrived and settled in, while Miss Emily Barton went into rooms in Lymstock kept by a former parlormaid ("my faithful Florence") and we were looked after by Miss Barton's present maid, Partridge, a grim but efficient personage who was assisted by a daily "girl."

As soon as we had been given a few days to settle down, Lymstock came solemnly to call. Everybody in Lymstock had a label—"rather like happy families" as Joanna said. There was Mr. Symmington the lawyer, thin and dry, with his querulous bridge-playing wife. Dr. Griffith—the dark, melancholy doctor—and his sister who was big and hearty. The vicar, a scholarly absent-minded elderly man and his erratic eager-faced wife. Rich dilettante Mr. Pye of Prior's End, and finally Miss Emily Barton herself, the perfect spinster of village tradition.

Joanna fingered the cards with something like awe. "I didn't know," she said in an awestruck voice, "that people really *called*—with *cards!*"

"That," I told her, "is because you know nothing about the country."

Joanna is very pretty and very gay, and she likes dancing and cocktails and love affairs and rushing about in high-powered cars. She is definitely and entirely urban.

"At any rate," said Joanna, "I look all right."

I studied her critically and was not able to agree.

Joanna was dressed (by Mirotin) for le sport. The effect was quite charming, but a bit startling for Lymstock.

"No," I said. "You're all wrong. You ought to

be wearing an old faded tweed skirt with a nice cashmere jumper matching it and perhaps a rather baggy cardigan coat, and you'd wear a felt hat and thick stockings and old well-worn brogues. Your face is all wrong, too," I added.

"What's wrong with that? I've got on my Country Tan Make-Up No. 2."

"Exactly," I said. "If you lived here, you would have just a little powder to take the shine off the nose and you would almost certainly be wearing all your eyebrows instead of only a quarter of them."

Joanna laughed, and said that coming to the country was a new experience and she was going to enjoy it.

"I'm afraid you'll be terribly bored," I said remorsefully.

"No, I shan't. I really was fed up with all my crowd, and though you won't be sympathetic I really was very cut up about Paul. It will take me a long time to get over it."

I was skeptical over this. Joanna's love affairs always run the same course. She has a mad infatuation for some completely spineless young man who is a misunderstood genius. She listens to his endless complaints and works to get him recognition. Then, when he is ungrateful, she is deeply wounded and says her heart is broken—until the next gloomy young man comes along, which is usually about three weeks later.

I did not take Joanna's broken heart very seriously, but I did see that living in the country was like a new game to my attractive sister. She entered with zest into the pastime of returning calls. We duly received invitations to tea and to bridge, which we accepted, and issued invitations in our turn.

To us, it was all novel and entertaining—a new game.

And, as I say, when the anonymous letter came, it struck me, at first, as amusing too.

For a minute or two after opening the letter, I stared at it uncomprehendingly. Printed words had been cut out and pasted on a sheet of paper.

The letter, using terms of the coarsest character, expressed the writer's opinion that Joanna and I were not brother and sister.

"Hullo," said Joanna. "What is it?"

"It's a particularly foul anonymous letter," I said.

I was still suffering from shock. Somehow one didn't expect that kind of thing in the placid backwater of Lymstock.

Joanna at once displayed lively interest. "*No*? What does it say?"

In novels, I have noticed, anonymous letters of a foul and disgusting character are never shown, if possible, to women. It is implied that women must at all cost be shielded from the shock it might give their delicate nervous systems.

I am sorry to say it never occurred to me not to show the letter to Joanna. I handed it to her at once.

She vindicated my belief in her toughness by displaying no emotion but that of amusement. "What an awful bit of dirt! I've always heard about anonymous letters, but I've never seen one before. Are they always like this?"

"I can't tell you," I said. "It's my first experience, too."

Joanna began to giggle. "You must have been right about my make-up, Jerry. I suppose they think I just *must* be an abandoned female!"

"That," I said, "coupled with the fact that our father was a tall, dark, lantern-jawed man and our mother a fair-haired blue-eyed little creature, and that I take after him and you take after her."

Joanna nodded thoughtfully. "Yes, we're not a bit alike. Nobody would take us for brother and sister."

"Somebody certainly hasn't," I said with feeling.

Joanna said she thought it was frightfully funny. She dangled the letter thoughtfully by one corner and asked what we were to do with it.

"The correct procedure, I believe," I said, "is to drop it into the fire with a sharp exclamation of disgust."

I suited the action to the word, and Joanna applauded. "You did that beautifully," she said. "You ought to have been on the stage. It's lucky we still have fires, isn't it?"

"The waste-paper basket would have been much less dramatic," I agreed. "I could, of course, have set light to it with a match and slowly watched it burn—or watched it slowly burn."

"Things never burn when you want them to," said Joanna. "They go out. You'd probably have had to strike match after match."

She got up and went toward the window. Then, standing there, she turned her head sharply. "I wonder," she said, "who wrote it?"

"We're never likely to know," I said.

"No—I suppose not." She was silent a moment, and then said: "I don't know when I come to think of it that it is so funny after all. You know, I thought they—they *liked* us down here."

"So they do," I said. "This is just some half-crazy brain on the borderline."

"I suppose so. Ugh—nasty!"

As she went out into the sunshine I thought to myself as I smoked my after-breakfast cigarette that she was quite right. It *was* nasty. Someone resented our coming here—someone resented Joanna's bright young sophisticated beauty—someone wanted to *hurt*. To take it with a laugh was perhaps the best way—but deep down it wasn't funny.

Dr. Griffith came that morning. I had fixed up for him to give me a weekly overhaul. I liked Owen Griffith. He was dark, ungainly, with awkward ways of moving and deft very gentle hands. He had a jerky way of talking and was rather shy.

He reported progress to be encouraging. Then he added, "You're feeling all right, aren't you? Is it my fancy, or are you a bit under the weather this morning?"

"Not really," I said. "A particularly scurrilous anonymous letter arrived with the morning coffee, and it's left rather a nasty taste in the mouth."

He dropped his bag on the floor. His thin dark face was excited. "Do you mean to say that *you've* had one of them?"

I was interested. "They've been going about, then?"

"Yes. For some time."

"Oh," I said. "I see. I was under the impression that our presence as strangers was resented here."

"No, no, it's nothing to do with that. It's

just—" He paused and then asked, "What did it say? At least"—he turned suddenly red and embarrassed—"perhaps I oughtn't to ask?"

"I'll tell you with pleasure," I said. "It just said that the fancy tart I'd brought down with me wasn't my sister—not 'alf! And that, I may say, is a shortened version."

His dark face flushed angrily. "How damnable! Your sister didn't—she's not upset, I hope?"

"Joanna," I said, "looks a little like the angel off the top of the Christmas tree, but she's eminently modern and quite tough. She found it highly entertaining. Such things haven't come her way before."

"I should hope not, indeed," said Griffith warmly.

"And anyway," I said firmly, "that's the best way to take it, I think. As something utterly ridiculous."

"Yes," said Owen Griffith, "only—"

He stopped, and I chimed in quickly. "Quite so," I said. "Only is the word!"

"The trouble is," he said, "that this sort of thing, once it starts, *grows*."

"So I should imagine."

"It's pathological, of course."

I nodded. "Any idea who's behind it?" I asked.

"No, I wish I had. You see, the anonymous letter pest arises from one of two causes. Either it's *particular*—directed at one person or set of people, that is to say it's *motivated*, it's someone who's got a definite grudge (or thinks he has) and who chooses a particularly nasty and underhand way of working it off. It's mean and disgusting but it's not necessarily crazy, and it's usually fairly easy to trace the writer—a discharged servant, a jealous woman, and so on. But if it's *general*, and not particular, then it's more serious.

"The letters are sent indiscriminately and serve the purpose of working off some frustration in the writer's mind. As I say, it's definitely pathological. And the craze grows. In the end, of course, you track down the person in question—(it's often someone extremely unlikely) and that's that. There was a bad outburst of the kind over the other side of the county last year—turned out to be the head of the millinery department in a big draper's establishment. Quiet, refined woman— had been there for years.

"I remember something of the same kind in my last practice up north. But that turned out to be purely personal spite. Still, as I say, I've seen something of this kind of thing, and, quite frankly, it frightens me!"

"Has it been going on long?" I asked.

"I don't think so. Hard to say, of course, because people who get these letters don't go round advertising the fact. They put them in the fire."

He paused.

"I've had one myself. Symmington, the solicitor, he's had one. And one or two of my poorer patients have told me about them."

"All much the same sort of thing?"

"Oh, yes. A definite harping on the sex theme. That's always a feature." He grinned. "Symmington was accused of illicit relations with his lady clerk—poor old Miss Ginch, who's forty at least, with pince-nez and teeth like a rabbit. Symmington took it straight to the police. My letters accused me of violating professional decorum with my lady patients, stressing the details. They're all quite childish and absurd, but horribly venomous." His face changed, grew grave. "But all the same, I'm *afraid*. These things can be *dangerous*, you know."

"I suppose they can."

"You see," he said, "crude, childish spite though it is, sooner or later *one of these letters will hit the mark*. And then, God knows what may happen! I'm afraid, too, of the effect upon the slow, suspicious, uneducated mind. If they see a thing written, they believe it's true. All sorts of complications may arise."

"It was an illiterate sort of letter," I said thoughtfully, "written by somebody practically illiterate, I should say."

"Was it?" said Owen and went away.

Thinking it over afterward, I found that "Was it?" rather disturbing.

I am not going to pretend that the arrival of our anonymous letter did not leave a nasty taste in the mouth. It did. At the same time, it soon passed out of my mind. I did not, you see, at that point, take it seriously. I think I remember saying to myself that these things probably happen fairly often in out-of-the-way villages. Some hysterical woman with a taste for dramatizing herself was probably at the bottom of it. Anyway, if the letters were as childish and silly as the one we had got, they couldn't do much harm.

The next *incident*, if I may put it so, occurred about a week later, when Partridge, her lips set tightly together, informed me that Beatrice, the daily help, would not be coming today.

"I gather, sir," said Partridge, "that the girl has been upset."

I was not very sure what Partridge was implying, but I diagnosed (wrongly) some stomach trouble to which Partridge was too delicate to allude more directly. I said I was sorry and hoped she would soon be better.

"The girl is perfectly well, sir," said Partridge. "She is upset in her feelings."

"Oh," I said rather doubtfully.

"Owing," went on Partridge, "to a letter she has received. Making, I understand, insinuations."

The grimness of Partridge's eye made me apprehensive that the insinuations were concerned with me. Since I could hardly have recognized Beatrice by sight if I had met her in the town, so unaware of her had I been, I felt a not unnatural annoyance. An invalid hobbling about on two sticks is hardly cast for the role of deceiver of village girls.

I said irritably, "What nonsense!"

"My very words, sir, to the girl's mother," said Partridge. " 'Goings-on in this house,' I said to her, 'there never have been and never will be while I am in charge. As to Beatrice,' I said, 'girls are different nowadays, and as to goings-on elsewhere I can say nothing.' But the truth is, sir, that Beatrice's friend from the garage as she walks out with got one of them nasty letters, too, and he isn't acting reasonable at all."

"I have never heard anything so preposterous in my life," I said angrily.

"It's my opinion, sir," said Partridge, "that

we're well rid of the girl. What I say is, she wouldn't take on so if there wasn't *something* she didn't want found out. No smoke without fire, that's what I say."

I had no idea how horribly tired I was going to get of that particular phrase.

That morning, by way of adventure, I was to walk down to the village. The sun was shining, the air was cool and crisp and with the sweetness of spring in it. I assembled my sticks and started off, firmly refusing to permit Joanna to accompany me.

It was arranged that she should pick me up with the car and drive me back up the hill in time for lunch.

"That ought to give you time to pass the time of day with everyone in Lymstock."

"I have no doubt," I said, "that I shall have seen anybody who is anybody by then."

For morning in the High Street was a kind of rendezvous for shoppers, when news was exchanged.

I did not, after all, walk down to the town unaccompanied. I had gone about two hundred yards, when I heard a bicycle bell behind me, then a scrunching of brakes, and then Megan Hunter more or less fell off her machine at my feet.

"Hullo," she said breathlessly as she rose and dusted herself off.

I rather liked Megan and always felt oddly sorry for her.

She was Symmington the lawyer's stepdaughter, Mrs. Symmington's daughter by a first marriage. Nobody talked much about Mr. (or Captain) Hunter, and I gathered that he was considered best forgotten. He was reported to have treated Mrs. Symmington very badly. She had divorced him a year or two after the marriage. She was a woman with means of her own and had settled down with her little daughter in Lymstock "to forget," and had eventually married the only eligible bachelor in the place, Richard Symmington.

There were two boys of the second marriage to whom their parents were devoted, and I fancied that Megan sometimes felt odd-man in the establishment. She certainly did not resemble her mother, who was a small anemic woman, fadedly pretty, who talked in a thin melancholy voice of servant difficulties and her health.

Megan was a tall awkward girl, and although she was actually twenty, she looked more like a schoolgirlish sixteen. She had a shock of untidy brown hair, hazel green eyes, a thin bony face, and an unexpectedly charming one-sided smile. Her clothes were drab and unattractive and she usually had on lisle-thread stockings with holes in them.

She looked, I decided this morning, much more like a horse than a human being. In fact, she would have been a very nice horse with a little grooming.

She spoke, as usual, in a kind of breathless rush:

"I've been up to the farm—you know, Lasher's —to see if they'd got any duck eggs. They've got an awfully nice lot of little pigs. Sweet! Do you like pigs? I do. I even like the smell."

"Well-kept pigs shouldn't smell," I said.

"Shouldn't they? They all do around here. Are you walking down to the town? I saw you were alone, so I thought I'd stop and walk with you, only I stopped rather suddenly.''

"You've torn your stocking," I said.

Megan looked rather ruefully at her right leg. ''So I have. But it's got two holes already, so it doesn't matter very much, does it?''

"Don't you ever mend your stockings, Megan?"

"Rather. When Mummie catches me. But she doesn't notice awfully what I do—so it's lucky in a way, isn't it?''

"You don't seem to realize you're grown up," I said.

"You mean I ought to be more like your sister? All dolled up?''

I rather resented this description of Joanna. "She looks clean and tidy and pleasing to the eye," I said.

"She's awfully pretty," said Megan. "She isn't a bit like you, is she? Why not?''

"Brothers and sisters aren't always alike.''

"No. Of course I'm not very like Brian or Colin. And Brian and Colin aren't like each other.'' She paused and said, "It's very rum, isn't it?''

"What is?''

Megan replied briefly:

"Families.''

I said thoughtfully, "I suppose they are.''

I wondered just what was passing in her mind. We walked on in silence for a moment or two, then Megan said in a rather shy voice, "You fly, don't you?''

"Yes.''

"That's how you got hurt?''

"Yes, I crashed.''

Megan said, "Nobody down here flies.''

"No," I said, "I suppose not. Would you like to fly, Megan?"

"Me?" Megan seemed surprised. "Goodness, no. I should be sick. I'm sick in a train even."

She paused and then asked with that directness which only a child usually displays: "Will you get all right and be able to fly again, or will you always be a bit of a crock?"

"My doctor says I shall be quite all right."

"Yes, but is he the kind of man who tells lies?"

"I don't think so," I replied. "In fact, I'm quite sure of it. I trust him."

"That's all right then. But a lot of people do tell lies."

I accepted this undeniable statement of fact in silence.

Megan said in a detached judicial kind of way, "I'm glad. I was afraid you looked bad-tempered because you were crocked up for life—but if it's just natural, it's different."

"I'm not bad-tempered," I said coldly.

"Well, irritable, then."

"I'm irritable because I'm in a hurry to get fit again—and these things can't be hurried."

"Then why fuss?"

I began to laugh. "My dear girl, aren't you ever in a hurry for things to happen?"

Megan considered the question. She said, "No. Why should I be? There's nothing to be in a hurry about. Nothing ever happens."

I was struck by something forlorn in the words. I said gently, "What do you do with yourself down here?"

She shrugged her shoulders. "What is there to do?"

"Haven't you any hobbies? Don't you play

games? Haven't you got friends around about?"

"I'm stupid at games. There aren't many girls around here, and the ones there are I don't like. They think I'm awful."

"Nonsense. Why should they?"

Megan shook her head.

We were now entering the High Street. Megan said sharply:

"Here's Miss Griffith coming. Hateful woman. She's always at me to join her foul Guides. I hate Guides. Why dress up and go about in clumps and put badges on yourself for something you haven't really learned to do properly. I think it's all rot."

On the whole I rather agreed with Megan. But Miss Griffith had descended upon us before I could voice any assent.

The doctor's sister, who rejoiced in the singularly inappropriate name of Aimée, had all the positive assurance her brother lacked. She was a handsome woman in a masculine weather-beaten way, with a deep voice.

"Hullo, you two," she bayed at us. "Gorgeous morning, isn't it? Megan, you're just the person I want to see. I want some help. Addressing envelopes for the Conservative Association."

Megan muttered something elusive, propped up her bicycle against the curb and dived in a purposeful way into the International Stores.

"Extraordinary child," said Miss Griffith, looking after her. "Bone lazy. Spends her time mooning about. Must be a great trial to poor Mrs. Symmington. I know her mother's tried more than once to get her to take up something—shorthand-typing, you know, or cookery, or keeping Angora rabbits. She needs an *interest* in life."

I thought that was probably true, but felt that in Megan's place I should have withstood firmly any of Aimée Griffith's suggestions for the simple reason that her aggressive personality would have put my back up.

"I don't believe in idleness," went on Miss Griffith. "And certainly not for young people. It's not as though Megan was pretty or attractive or anything like that. Sometimes I think the girl's half-witted. A great disappointment to her mother. The father, you know," she lowered her voice slightly, "was definitely a wrong 'un. Afraid the child takes after him. Painful for her mother. Oh, well, it takes all sorts to make a world, that's what I say."

"Fortunately," I responded.

Aimée Griffith gave a "jolly" laugh.

"Yes, it wouldn't do if we were all made to one pattern. But I don't like to see anyone not getting all he can out of life. I enjoy life myself and I want everyone to enjoy it too. People say to me you must be bored to death living down there in the country all the year around. Not a bit of it, I say. I'm always busy, always happy! There's always something going on in the country. My time's taken up, what with my Guides, and the Institute and various committees—to say nothing of looking after Owen."

At this minute, Miss Griffith saw an acquaintance on the other side of the street, and uttering a bay of recognition she leaped across the road, leaving me free to pursue my course to the bank.

I always found Miss Griffith rather overwhelming.

•　•　•

My business at the bank transacted satisfac-
torily, I went on to the offices of Messrs.
Galbraith, Galbraith and Symmington. I don't
know if there were any Galbraith's extant. I never
saw any. I was shown into Richard Symmington's
inner office which had the agreeable mustiness of
a long-established legal firm.

Vast numbers of deed boxes labeled Lady
Hope, Sir Everard Carr, William Yatesby-Hoares
Esq., Deceased, etc., gave the required atmosphere of decorous county families and legitimate,
long-established business.

Studying Mr. Symmington as he bent over the
documents I had brought, it occurred to me that if
Mrs. Symmington had encountered disaster in her
first marriage, she had certainly played safe in her
second. Richard Symmington was the acme of
calm respectability, the sort of man who would
never give his wife a moment's anxiety. A long
neck with a pronounced Adam's apple, a slightly
cadaverous face and a long thin nose. A kindly
man, no doubt, a good husband and father, but
not one to set the pulses madly racing.

Presently Mr. Symmington began to speak. He
spoke clearly and slowly, delivering himself of
much good sense and shrewd acumen. We settled
the matter in hand and I rose to go, remarking as I
did so, "I walked down the hill with your stepdaughter."

For a moment Mr. Symmington looked as
though he did not know who his stepdaughter
was, then he smiled.

"Oh, yes, of course—Megan. She—er—has
been back from school some time. We're thinking
about finding her something to do—yes, to do.

But, of course, she's very young still. And backward for her age, so they say. Yes, so they tell me.''

I went out. In the outer office was a very old man on a stool writing slowly and laboriously, a small, cheeky-looking boy and a middle-aged woman with frizzy hair and pince-nez who was typing with some speed and dash.

If this was Miss Ginch I agreed with Owen Griffith that tender passages between her and her employer were exceedingly unlikely.

I went into the baker's and said my piece about the currant loaf. It was received with the exclamations and incredulity proper to the occasion, and a new currant loaf was thrust upon me in replacement—"fresh from the oven this minute"—as its indecent heat pressed against my chest proclaimed to be no less than truth.

I came out of the shop and looked up and down the street, hoping to see Joanna with the car. The walk had tired me a good deal and it was awkward getting along with my sticks and the currant loaf.

But there was no sign of Joanna as yet.

Suddenly my eyes were held in glad and incredulous surprise. Along the pavement toward me there came floating a goddess. There is really no other word for it. The perfect features, the crisply curling golden hair, the tall exquisitely shaped body. And she walked like a goddess, without effort, seeming to swim nearer and near. A glorious, an incredible, a breath-taking girl!

In my intense excitement something had to go. What went was the currant loaf. It slipped from my clutches. I made a dive after it and lost my stick, which clattered to the pavement, and I slipped and nearly fell myself.

It was the strong arm of the goddess that caught and held me.

I began to stammer: "Th-thanks awfully, I'm f-f-frightfully sorry."

She had retrieved the currant loaf and handed it to me together with the stick. And then she smiled kindly and said cheerfully, "Don't mention it. No trouble, I assure you," and the magic died completely before the flat, competent voice.

A nice, healthy-looking, well set-up girl; no more.

I fell to reflecting what would have happened if the gods had given Helen of Troy exactly those flat accents. How strange that a girl could trouble your inmost soul so long as she kept her mouth shut, and that the moment she spoke the glamor could vanish as though it had never been.

I had known the reverse happen, though. I had seen a little sad monkey-faced woman whom no one would turn to look at twice. Then she had opened her mouth and suddenly enchantment had lived and bloomed and Cleopatra had cast her spell anew.

Joanna had drawn up at the curb beside me without my noticing her arrival. She asked if there was anything the matter.

"Nothing," I said, pulling myself together. "I was reflecting on Helen of Troy and others."

"What a funny place to do it," said Joanna. "You looked *most* odd, standing there clasping currant bread to your breast with your mouth wide open."

"I've had a shock," I said. "I had been transplanted to Ilium and back again."

I added, indicating a retreating back that was

swimming gracefully away, "Do you know who that is?"

Peering after the girl Joanna said that it was Elsie Holland, the Symmington's nursery governess.

"Is that what struck you all of a heap?" she asked. "She's good-looking, but a bit of a wet fish."

"I know," I said. "Just a nice kind girl. And I'd been thinking her Aphrodite."

Joanna opened the door of the car and I got in.

"It's funny, isn't it?" she said. "Some people have lots of looks and absolutely no S. A. That girl hasn't. It seems such a pity."

I said that if she was a nursery governess it was probably just as well.

That afternoon we went to tea with Mr. Pye.

Mr. Pye was an extremely ladylike plump little man, devoted to his *petit point* chairs, his Dresden shepherdesses and his collection of period furniture. He lived at Prior's Lodge in the grounds of which were the ruins of the old Priory dissolved at the Reformation.

It was hardly a man's house. The curtains and cushions were of pastel shades in the most expensive silks.

Mr. Pye's small plump hands quivered with excitement as he described and exhibited his treasures, and his voice rose to a falsetto squeak as he narrated the exciting circumstances in which he had brought his Italian bedstead home from Verona.

Joanna and I, both being fond of antiques, met with approval.

"It is really a pleasure, a great pleasure, to have

such an acquisition to our little community. The dear good people down here, you know, so painfully bucolic—not to say *provincial*. Vandals—absolute vandals! And the insides of their houses—it would make you weep, dear lady, I assure you it would make you weep. Perhaps it has done so?''

Joanna said she hadn't gone quite as far as that.

''The house you have taken,'' went on Mr. Pye, ''Miss Emily Barton's house. Now that is charming, and she has some quite nice pieces. Quite nice. One or two of them are really first-class. And she has taste, too—although I'm not quite so sure of that as I was. Sometimes, I am afraid, I think it's really sentiment. She likes to keep things as they were—but not for *le bon motif*—not because of the resultant harmony—but because it is the way her mother had them.''

He transferred his attention to me, and his voice changed. It altered from that of the rapt artist to that of the born gossip:

''You didn't know the family at all? No, quite so—yes, through house agents. But, my dears, you *ought* to have known that family! When I came here the old mother was still alive. An incredible person—quite incredible! A *monster,* if you know what I mean. Positively a monster. The old-fashioned Victorian monster, devouring her young. Yes, that's what it amounted to. She was monumental, you know, must have weighed seventeen stone, and all the five daughters revolved around her. 'The girls!' That's how she always spoke of them. The girls! And the eldest was well over sixty then.

'' 'Those stupid girls!' she used to call them sometimes. Black slaves, that's all they were, fetching and carrying and agreeing with her. Ten o'clock they had to go to bed and they weren't allowed a fire in their bedroom, and as for asking their own friends to the house, that would have been unheard of. She despised them, you know, for not getting married, and yet so arranged their lives that it was practically impossible for them to meet anybody. I believe Emily, or perhaps it was Agnes, did have some kind of affair with a curate. But his family wasn't good enough and Mamma soon put a stop to *that!*"

"It sounds like a novel," said Joanna.

"Oh, my dear, it was. And then the dreadful old woman died, but of course, it was far too late *then*. They just went on living there and talking in hushed voices about what poor Mamma would have wished. Even repapering her bedroom they felt to be quite sacrilegious. Still they did enjoy themselves in the parish in a quiet way. . . . But none of them had much stamina, and they just died off one by one. Influenza took off Edith, and Minnie had an operation and didn't recover and poor Mable had a stroke—Emily looked after her in the most devoted manner. Really that poor woman has done nothing but nursing for the last ten years. A charming creature, don't you think? Like a piece of Dresden. So sad for her having financial anxieties—but of course, all investments have depreciated."

"We feel rather awful being in her house," said Joanna.

"No, no, my dear young lady. You musn't feel that way. Her dear good Florence is devoted to her and she told me herself how happy she was to have got such nice tenants." Here Mr. Pye made a little bow. "She told me she thought she had been most fortunate."

"The house," I said, "has a very soothing atmosphere."

Mr. Pye darted a quick glance at me.

"Really? You feel that? Now, that's very interesting. I wondered, you know. Yes, I wondered."

"What do you mean, Mr. Pye?" asked Joanna.

Mr. Pye spread out his plump hands. "Nothing, nothing. One wondered, that is all. I do believe in atmosphere, you know. People's thoughts and feelings. They give their impression to the walls and the furniture."

I did not speak for a moment or two. I was looking around me and wondering how I would describe the atmosphere of Prior's Lodge. It seemed to me that the curious thing was that it hadn't any atmosphere! That was really very remarkable.

I reflected on this point so long that I heard nothing of the conversation going on between Joanna and her host. I was recalled to myself, however, by hearing Joanna uttering farewell preliminaries. I came out of my dream and added my quota.

We all went out into the hall. As we came toward the front door a letter came through the box and fell on the mat.

"Afternoon post," murmured Mr. Pye as he picked it up. "Now, my dear young people, you will come again, won't you? Such a pleasure to meet some broader minds, if you understand me, in this peaceful backwater where nothing ever happens."

Shaking hands with us twice over, he helped me

with exaggerated care into the car. Joanna took the wheel, she negotiated with some care the circular sweep around a plot of unblemished grass, then with a straight drive ahead, she raised a hand to wave goodby to our host where he stood on the steps of the house. I leaned forward to do the same.

But our gesture of farewell went unheeded. Mr. Pye had opened his mail. He was standing staring down at the open sheet in his hand.

Joanna had described him once as a plump pink cherub. He was still plump, but he was not looking like a cherub now. His face was a dark congested purple, contorted with rage and surprise. Yes, and fear, too.

And at that moment I realized that there had been something familiar about the look of that envelope. I had not realized it at the time—indeed, it had been one of those things that you note unconsciously without knowing that you do note them.

"Goodness," said Joanna, "what's bitten the poor pet?"

"I rather fancy," I said, "that it's the Hidden Hand again."

She turned an astonished face toward me and the car swerved.

"Careful, wench," I said.

Joanna refixed her attention on the road. She was frowning. "You mean a letter like the one you got."

"That's my guess."

"What is this place?" asked Joanna. "It looks the most innocent, sleepy harmless little bit of England you can imagine."

"Where, to quote Mr. Pye, nothing ever happens," I cut in. "He chose the wrong minute to say that. Something has happened."

"Jerry," said Joanna. "I—I don't think I like this." For the first time, there was a note of fear in her voice.

I did not answer, for I, too, did not like it. . . .

Such a peaceful smiling happy countryside—and down underneath something evil. . . .

It was as though at that moment I had a premonition of all that was to come. . . .

The days passed. We went and played bridge at the Symmingtons and Mrs. Symmington annoyed me a good deal by the way she referred to Megan.

"The poor child's so awkward. They are at that age, when they've left school and before they are properly grown up."

Joanna said sweetly, "But Megan's twenty, isn't she?"

"Oh, yes, yes. But of course, she's very young for her age. Quite a child still. It's so nice, I think, when girls don't grow up too quickly." She laughed. "I expect all mothers want their children to remain babies."

"I can't think why," said Joanna. "After all, it would be a bit awkward if one had a child who remained mentally six while his body grew up."

Mrs. Symmington looked annoyed and said Miss Burton mustn't take things so literally.

I was pleased with Joanna, and it occurred to me that I did not really much care for Mrs. Symmington. That anemic middle-aged prettiness concealed, I thought, a selfish, grasping nature.

Joanna asked maliciously if Mrs. Symmington were going to give a dance for Megan.

"A dance?" Mrs. Symmington seemed surprised and amused. "Oh, no, we don't do things like that down here."

"I see. Just tennis parties and things like that."

"Our tennis court has not been played on for years. Neither Richard nor I play. I suppose, later, when the boys grow up—oh, Megan will find plenty to do. She's quite happy just pottering about, you know. Let me see, did I deal? Two no trumps."

As we drove home, Joanna said with a vicious pressure on the accelerator pedal that made the car leap forward, "I feel awfully sorry for that girl."

"Megan?"

"Yes. Her mother doesn't like her."

"Oh, come now, Joanna, it's not as bad as that."

"Yes, it is. Lots of mothers don't like their children. Megan, I should imagine, is an awkward sort of creature to have about the house. She disturbs the pattern—the Symmington pattern. It's a complete unit without her—and that's a most unhappy feeling for a sensitive creature to have—and she *is* sensitive."

"Yes," I said, "I think she is."

I was silent for a moment.

Joanna suddenly laughed mischievously. "Bad luck for you about the governess."

"I don't know what you mean," I said with dignity.

"Nonsense. Masculine chagrin was written on your face every time you looked at her. I agree with you, it is a waste. And I don't see who else there is here for you. You'll have to fall back upon Aimée Griffith."

"God forbid," I said with a shudder. "And

anyway," I added, "why all this concern about my love life? What about you, my girl? You'll need a little distraction down here, if I know you. No unappreciated genius, knocking about here. You'll have to fall back on Owen Griffith. He's the only unattached male in the place."

Joanna tossed her head. "Dr. Griffith doesn't like me."

"He's not seen much of you."

"He's seen enough apparently to make him cross over if he sees me coming along the High Street!"

"A most unusual reaction," I said sympathetically. "And one you're not used to."

Joanna drove in silence through the gate of Little Furze and around to the garage. Then she said, "There may be something in that idea of yours. I don't see why any man should deliberately cross the street to avoid me. It's rude apart from everything else."

"I see," I said. "You're going to hunt the man down in cold blood."

"Well, I don't like being avoided."

I got slowly and carefully out of the car and balanced my sticks. Then I offered my sister a piece of advice:

"Let me tell you this, girl. Owen Griffith isn't any of your tame, whining, artistic young men. Unless you're careful, you'll stir up a hornets' nest about your ears. That man could be dangerous."

"Oh, do you think so?" demanded Joanna with every symptom of pleasure at the prospect.

"Leave the poor devil alone," I said sternly.

"How dare he cross the street when he saw me coming?"

"All you women are alike. You harp on one theme. You'll have sister Aimée gunning for you, too, if I'm not mistaken."

"She dislikes me already," said Joanna. She spoke meditatively, but with a certain satisfaction.

"We have come down here," I said sternly, "for peace and quiet, and I mean to see we get it."

But peace and quiet were the last things we were to have.

2

It was about a week later that I came back to the house to find Megan sitting on the veranda steps, her chin resting on her knees.

She greeted me with her usual lack of ceremony. "Hullo," she said. "Do you think I could come to lunch?"

"Certainly," I said.

"If it's chops, or anything difficult like that and they won't go around, just tell me," shouted Megan as I went around to apprise Partridge of the fact that there would be three to lunch.

I fancy that Partridge sniffed. She certainly managed to convey without saying a word of any kind, that she didn't think much of that Miss Megan.

I went back to the veranda.

"Is it all right?" asked Megan anxiously.

"Quite all right," I said. "Irish stew."

"Oh, well, that's rather like dogs' dinner any-

way, isn't it? I mean it's mostly potato an‿
flavor.''

"Quite," I said.

We were silent while I smoked my pipe. It was
quite a companionable silence.

Megan broke it by saying suddenly and violently, "I suppose you think I'm awful like everyone else."

I was so startled that my pipe fell out of my
mouth. It was a meerschaum, just coloring nicely,
and it broke. I said angrily to Megan, "Now see
what you've done."

That most unaccountable of children, instead of
being upset, merely grinned broadly. "I do like
you," she said.

It was a most warming remark. It is the remark
that one fancies perhaps erroneously that one's
dog would say if he could talk. It occurred to me
that Megan, for all she looked like a horse had the
disposition of a dog. She was certainly not quite
human.

"What did you say before the catastrophe?" I
asked, carefully picking up the fragments of my
cherished pipe.

"I said I supposed you thought me awful," said
Megan but not at all in the same tone she had said
it before.

"Why should I?"

Megan said gravely, "Because I am."

I said sharply, "Don't be stupid."

Megan shook her head. "That's just it. I'm not
really stupid. People think I am. They don't know
that inside I know just what they're like, and that
all the time I'm hating them."

"*Hating* them?"

"Yes," said Megan.

Her eyes, those melancholy, unchildlike eyes stared straight into mine, without blinking. It was a long, mournful gaze.

"You would hate people if you were like me," she said. "If you weren't wanted."

"Don't you think you're being rather morbid?" I asked.

"Yes," said Megan. "That's what people always say when you're saying the truth. And it is true. I'm not wanted and I can quite see why. Mummie doesn't like me a bit. I remind her, I think, of my father, who was cruel to her and pretty dreadful from all I can hear. Only mothers can't say they don't want their children and just go away. Or eat them. Cats eat the kittens they don't like. Awfully sensible, I think. No waste or mess. But human mothers have to keep their children, and look after them. It hasn't been so bad while I could be sent away to school—but you see what Mummie would really like is to be just herself and my stepfather and the boys."

I said slowly, "I·still think you're morbid, Megan, but accepting some of what you say as true, why don't you go away and have a life of your own?"

She gave me an odd unchildlike smile. "You mean take up a career. Earn my living?"

"Yes."

"What at?"

"You could train for something, I suppose. Shorthand, typing, bookkeeping."

"I don't believe I could. I am stupid about doing things. And besides—"

"Well?"

She had turned her head away, now she turned it slowly back again. It was crimson and there were tears in her eyes. She spoke now with all the childishness back in her voice:

"Why should I go away? And be made to go away? They don't want me, but I'll *stay.* I'll stay and make everyone sorry. I'll make them all sorry. Hateful pigs! I hate everyone here in Lymstock. They all think I'm stupid and ugly. I'll show them! I'll show them! I'll—"

It was a childish, oddly pathetic rage.

I heard a step on the gravel around the corner of the house.

"Get up," I said savagely. "Go into the house through the drawing room. Go up to the bathroom. Wash your face. Quick."

She sprang awkwardly to her feet and darted through the window as Joanna came around the corner of the house.

I told her Megan had come to lunch.

"Good," said Joanna. "I like Megan, though I rather think she's a changeling. Something left on a doorstep by the fairies. But she's interesting."

I see that so far I have made little mention of the Reverend and Mrs. Calthrop.

And yet both the vicar and his wife were distinct personalities. Dane Calthrop himself was perhaps a being more remote from everyday life than anyone I have ever met. His existence was in his books and in his study. Mrs. Dane Calthrop, on the other hand, was quite terrifyingly on the spot. Though she seldom gave advice and never interfered, yet she represented to the uneasy consciences of the village the Deity personified.

She stopped me in the High Street the day after Megan had come to lunch. I had the usual feeling of surprise, because Mrs. Dane Calthrop's progress resembled coursing more than walking, thus according with her startling resemblance to a greyhound, and as her eyes were always fixed on the distant horizon you felt sure that her real objective was about a mile and a half away.

"Oh!" she said. "Mr. Burton!"

She said it rather triumphantly, as someone might who had solved a particularly clever puzzle. I admitted that I was Mr. Burton and Mrs. Dane Calthrop stopped focusing on the horizon and seemed to be trying to focus on me instead.

"Now what," she said, "did I want to see you about?"

I could not help her there. She stood frowning, deeply perplexed. "Something rather nasty," she said.

"I'm sorry about that," I said startled.

"Ah," cried Mrs. Dane Calthrop. "*Anonymous letters!* What's this story you've brought down here about anonymous letters?"

"I didn't bring it," I said, "it was here already."

"Nobody got any until you came, though," said Mrs. Dane Calthrop accusingly.

"But they did, Mrs. Dane Calthrop. The trouble had already started."

"Oh, dear," said Mrs. Dane Calthrop. "I don't like that."

She stood there, her eyes absent and far away again. She said:

"I can't help feeling it's all *wrong*. We're not like that here. Envy, of course, and malice, and all the mean spiteful little sins—but I didn't think there was anyone who would do that. No, I really didn't. And it distresses me, you see, because *I* ought to know."

Her fine eyes came back from the horizon and met mine. They were worried, and seemed to hold the honest bewilderment of a child's.

"Why ought you to know?" I said.

"I usually do. I've always felt that's my function. Caleb preaches good sound doctrine and administers the sacraments. That's a priest's duty, but if you admit marriage at all for a priest, then I think his wife's duty is to know what people are feeling and thinking, even if she can't do anything about it. And I haven't the least idea whose mind is—"

She broke off, adding absently, "They are such silly letters, too."

"Have you—er—had any yourself?"

I was a little diffident of asking, but Mrs. Dane Calthrop replied perfectly naturally, her eyes opening a little wider:

"Oh, yes, two—no, three. I forget exactly what they said. Something very silly about Caleb and the schoolmistress, I think. Quite absurd, because Caleb has absolutely no taste for flirtation. He never has had. So lucky being a clergyman."

"Quite," I said, "oh, quite."

"Caleb would have been a saint," said Mrs. Dane Calthrop, "if he hadn't been just a little too intellectual."

I did not feel qualified to answer this criticism, and anyway Mrs. Dane Calthrop went on, leaping back from her husband to the letters in rather a puzzling way.

"There are so many things the letters might say, but don't. That's what is so curious."

"I should hardly have thought they erred on the side of restraint," I said bitterly.

"But they don't seem to *know* anything. None of the real things."

"You mean?"

Those fine vague eyes met mine.

"Well, of course. There's plenty of wrongdoing here—any amount of shameful secrets. Why doesn't the writer use those?" She paused and then asked abruptly, "What did they say in your letter?"

"They suggested that my sister wasn't my sister."

"And she is?"

Mrs. Dane Calthrop asked the question with unembarrassed friendly interest.

"Certainly Joanna is my sister."

Mrs. Dane Calthrop nodded her head. "That just shows you what I mean. I daresay there are other things—"

Her clear uninterested eyes looked at me thoughtfully, and I suddenly understood why Lymstock was afraid of Mrs. Dane Calthrop.

In everybody's life there are hidden chapters which they hope may never be known. I felt that Mrs. Dane Calthrop knew them.

For once in my life, I was positively delighted when Aimée Griffith's hearty voice boomed out:

"Hullo, Maud. Glad I've just caught you. I want to suggest an alteration of date for the Sale of Work. Morning, Mr. Burton."

She went on:

"I must just pop into the grocer's and leave my order, then I'll come along to the Institute if that suits you?"

"Yes, yes, that will do quite well," said Mrs. Dane Calthrop.

Aimée Griffith went into the International Stores.

Mrs. Dane Calthrop said, "Poor thing."

I was puzzled. Surely she could not be pitying Aimée?

She went on, however: "You know, Mr. Burton, I'm rather afraid—"

"About this letter business?"

"Yes, you see it means—it must mean—" She paused, lost in thought, her eyes screwed up. Then she said slowly, as one who solves a problem, "Blind hatred . . . yes, blind hatred. But even a blind man might stab to the heart by pure chance. . . . And what would happen then, Mr. Burton?"

We were to know that before another day had passed.

Partridge, who enjoys calamity, came into Joanna's room at an early hour the following morning, and told her with considerable relish that Mrs. Symmington had committed suicide on the preceding afternoon.

Joanna, who had been lost in the mists of sleep, sat up in bed shocked wide awake.

"Oh, Partridge, how awful."

"Awful it is, Miss. It's wickedness taking your own life. Not but what she was drove to it, poor soul."

Joanna had an inkling of the truth then. She felt rather sick.

"Not—?" Her eyes questioned Partridge and Partridge nodded.

"That's right, Miss. One of them nasty letters."

"How beastly," said Joanna. "How absolutely beastly! All the same, I don't see why she should kill herself for a letter like that."

"Looks as though what was in the letter was true, Miss."

"What was in it?"

But that, Partridge couldn't or wouldn't say. Joanna came in to me, looking white and shocked. It seemed worse, somehow, that Mrs. Symmington was not the kind of person you associated with tragedy.

Joanna suggested that we might ask Megan to come to us for a day or two. Elsie Holland, she said, would be all right with the children, but was the kind of person who would, almost certainly, drive Megan half mad.

I agreed. I could imagine Elsie Holland uttering platitude after platitude and suggesting innumerable cups of tea. A kindly creature but not the right person for Megan.

We drove down to the Symmingtons' house after breakfast. We were both of us a little nervous. Our arrival might look like sheer ghoulish curiosity. Luckily we met Owen Griffith just coming out. He greeted me with some warmth, his worried face lighting up.

"Oh, hullo, Burton, I'm glad to see you. What I was afraid would happen sooner or later has happened. A damnable business!"

"Good morning, Dr. Griffith," said Joanna, using the voice she keeps for one of our deafer aunts.

Griffith started and flushed. "Oh—oh, good morning, Miss Burton."

"I thought perhaps," said Joanna, "that you didn't see me."

Owen Griffith got redder still. His shyness enveloped him like a mantle. "I'm—I'm so sorry—

preoccupied—I didn't."

Joanna went on mercilessly.

"After all, I *am* life-size."

"Merely kit-kat," I said in a stern aside to her. Then I went on:

"My sister and I, Griffith, wondered whether it would be a good thing if the girl came and stopped with us for a day or two? What do you think? I don't want to butt in—but it must be rather grim for the poor child. What would Symmington feel about it, do you think?"

Griffith turned the idea over in his mind for a moment or two.

"I think it would be an excellent thing," he said at last. "She's a queer, nervous sort of girl, and it would be good for her to get away from the whole thing. Miss Holland is doing wonders—she's an excellent head on her shoulders, but she really has quite enough to do with the two children and Symmington himself. He's quite broken up— bewildered."

"It was"—I hesitated—"suicide?"

Griffith nodded.

"Oh, yes. No question of accident. She wrote, 'I can't go on,' on a scrap of paper. The letter must have come by yesterday afternoon's post. The envelope was down on the floor by her chair and the letter itself was screwed up into a ball and thrown into the fireplace."

"What did—"

I stopped, rather horrified at myself.

"I beg your pardon," I said.

Griffith gave a quick, unhappy smile.

"You needn't mind asking. That letter will have to be read at the inquest. No getting out of it, more's the pity. It was the usual kind of thing—

couched in the same foul style. The specific accusation was that the second boy, Colin, was not Symmington's child."

"Do you think that was true?" I exclaimed incredulously.

Griffith shrugged his shoulders.

"I've no means of forming a judgment. I've only been here five years. As far as I've ever seen, the Symmingtons were a placid, happy couple devoted to each other and their children. It's true that the boy doesn't particularly resemble his parents—he's got bright red hair, for one thing —but a child often throws back in appearance to a grandfather or grandmother."

"That lack of resemblance might have been what prompted the particular accusation. A foul and quite uncalled-for blow at a venture."

"But it happened to hit the bull's-eye," said Joanna. "After all, she wouldn't have killed herself otherwise, would she?"

Griffith said doubtfully:

"I'm not quite sure. She's been ailing in health for sometime—neurotic, hysterical. I've been treating her for a nervous condition. It's possible, I think, that the shock of receiving such a letter, couched in those terms, may have induced such a state of panic and despondency that she may have decided to take her life. She may have worked herself up to feel that her husband might not believe her if she denied the story, and the general shame and disgust might have worked upon her so powerfully as to unbalance her judgment temporarily."

"Suicide while of unsound mind," said Joanna.

"Exactly. I shall be quite justified, I think, in putting forward that point of view at the inquest."

Joanna and I went on into the house.

The front door was open and it seemed easier than ringing the bell, especially as we heard Elsie Holland's voice inside.

She was talking to Mr. Symmington who, huddled in a chair, was looking completely dazed.

"No, but really, Mr. Symmington, you must take something. You haven't had any breakfast, not what I call a proper breakfast, and nothing to eat last night, and what with the shock and all, you'll be getting ill yourself, and you'll need all your strength. The doctor said so before he left."

Symmington said in a toneless voice, "You're very kind, Miss Holland, but—"

"A nice cup of hot tea," said Elsie Holland, thrusting the beverage on him firmly.

Personally I should have given the poor devil a stiff whisky-and-soda. He looked as though he needed it. However he accepted the tea, and looking up at Elsie Holland:

"I can't thank you for all you've done and are doing, Miss Holland. You've been perfectly splendid."

The girl flushed and looked pleased.

"It's nice of you to say that, Mr. Symmington. You must let me do all I can to help. Don't worry about the children—I'll see to them, and I've got the servants calmed down, and if there's anything I can do, letter-writing or telephoning, don't hesitate to ask me."

"You're very kind," Symmington said again.

Elsie Holland, turning, caught sight of us and came hurrying out into the hall.

"Isn't it terrible?" she said in a hushed whisper.

I thought, as I looked at her, that she was really a very nice girl. Kind, competent, practical in an emergency. Her magnificent blue eyes were just faintly rimmed with pink, showing that she had been soft-hearted enough to shed tears for her employer's death.

"Can we speak to you a minute?" asked Joanna. "We don't want to disturb Mr. Symmington."

Elsie Holland nodded comprehendingly and led the way into the dining room on the other side of the hall.

"It's been awful for him," she said. "Such a shock. Who ever would have thought a thing like this could happen? But of course, I do realize now that she had been queer for some time. Awfully nervous and weepy. I thought it was her health, though Dr. Griffith always said there was nothing really wrong with her. But she was snappy and irritable and some days you wouldn't know just how to take her."

"What we really came for," said Joanna, "was to know whether we could have Megan for a few days—that is, if she'd like to come."

Elsie Holland looked rather surprised.

"Megan?" she said doubtfully. "I don't know, I'm sure. I mean, it's ever so kind of you, but she's such a queer girl. One never knows what she's going to say or feel about things."

Joanna said rather vaguely, "We thought it might be a help, perhaps."

"Oh, well, as far as that goes, it would. I mean, I've got the boys to look after (they're with cook just now) and poor Mr. Symmington—he really needs looking after as much as anyone, and such a lot to do and see to. I really haven't had time to say much to Megan. I think she's upstairs in the old nursery at the top of the house. She seems to

want to get away from everyone. I don't know
if—"

Joanna gave me the faintest of looks. I slipped
quickly out of the room and upstairs.

The old nursery was at the top of the house. I
opened the door and went in. The room downstairs had given on to the garden behind and the
blinds had not been down there. But in this room
which faced the road they were decorously drawn
down.

Through a dim gray gloom I saw Megan. She
was crouching on a divan set against the far wall,
and I was reminded at once of some terrified animal, hiding. She looked petrified with fear.

"Megan," I said.

I came forward, and unconsciously I adopted
the tone one does adopt when you want to re-
assure a frightened animal. I'm really surprised I
didn't hold out a carrot or a piece of sugar. I felt
like that.

She stared at me, but she did not move, and her
expression did not alter.

"Megan," I said again. "Joanna and I have
come to ask you if you would like to come and
stay with us for a little."

Her voice came hollowly out of the dim
twilight:

"Stay with you? In your house?"

"Yes."

"You mean, you'll take me away from here?"

"Yes, my dear."

Suddenly she began to shake all over. It was
frightening and very moving.

"Oh, do take me away! Please do. It's so awful,
being here, and feeling so wicked."

I came over to her and her hands fastened on my coat sleeve.

"I'm an awful coward. I didn't know what a coward I was."

"It's all right, funnyface," I said. "These things are a bit shattering. Come along."

"Can we go at once? Without waiting a minute?"

"Well, you'll have to put a few things together, I suppose."

"What sort of things? Why?"

"My dear girl," I said. "We can provide you with a bed and a bath and the rest of it, but I'm darned if I lend you my toothbrush."

She gave a very faint weak little laugh.

"I see. I think I'm stupid today. You mustn't mind. I'll go and pack some things. You—you won't go away? You'll wait for me?"

"I'll be on the mat."

"Thank you. Thank you very much. I'm sorry I'm so stupid. But you see it's rather dreadful when your mother dies."

"I know," I said.

I gave her a friendly pat on the back and she flashed me a grateful look and disappeared into a bedroom. I went on downstairs.

"I found Megan," I said. "She's coming."

"Oh, now, that *is* a good thing," exclaimed Elsie Holland. "It will take her out of herself. She's rather a nervy girl, you know. Difficult. It will be a great relief to feel I haven't got her on my mind as well as everything else. It's very kind of you, Miss Burton. I hope she won't be a nuisance. Oh, dear, there's the telephone. I must go and answer it. Mr. Symmington isn't fit."

She hurried out of the room.

Joanna said, "Quite the ministering angel!"

"You said that rather nastily," I observed. "She's a nice, kind girl, and obviously most capable."

"Most. And she knows it."

"This is unworthy of you, Joanna," I said.

"Meaning why shouldn't the girl do her stuff?"

"Exactly."

"I never can stand seeing people pleased with themselves," said Joanna. "It arouses all my worst instincts. How did you find Megan?"

"Crouching in a darkened room looking rather like a stricken gazelle."

"Poor kid. She was quite willing to come?"

"She leaped at it."

A series of thuds out in the hall announced the descent of Megan and her suitcase. I went out and took it from her.

Joanna, behind me, said urgently, "Come on. I've already refused some nice hot tea twice."

We went out to the car. It annoyed me that Joanna had to sling the suitcase in. I could get along with one stick now, but I couldn't do any athletic feats.

"Get in," I said to Megan.

She got in, I followed her. Joanna started the car and we drove off.

We got to Little Furze and went into the drawing room.

Megan dropped into a chair and burst into tears. She cried with the hearty fervor of a child —bawled, I think, is the right word. I left the room in search of a remedy. Joanna stood by feeling rather helpless, I think.

Presently I heard Megan say in a thick choked

voice, "I'm sorry for doing this. It seems idiotic."

Joanna said kindly, "Not at all. Have another handkerchief."

I gather she supplied the necesary article. I re-entered the room and handed Megan a brimming glass.

"What is it?"

"A cocktail," I said.

"Is it? Is it really?" Megan's tears were instantly dried. "I've never drunk a cocktail."

"Everything has to have a beginning," I said.

Megan sipped her drink gingerly, then a beaming smile spread over her face, she tilted her head back and gulped it down at a draught.

"It's lovely," she said. "Can I have another?"

"No," I said.

"Why not?"

"In about ten minutes you'll probably know."

"Oh!"

Megan transferred her attention to Joanna.

"I really am awfully sorry for having made such a nuisance of myself howling away like that. I can't think why. It seems awfully silly when I'm so glad to be here."

"That's all right," said Joanna. "We're very pleased to have you."

"You can't be really. It's just kindness on your part. But I am grateful."

"Please don't be grateful," said Joanna, "it will embarrass me. You're our friend and we're glad to have you here. That's all there is to it. . . ."

She took Megan upstairs to unpack.

Partridge came in, looking sour, and said she had made two cup custards for lunch and what should she do about it?

•   •   •

The inquest was held three days later.

The time of Mrs. Symmington's death was put at between three and four o'clock. She was alone in the house, Symmington was at his office, the maids were having their day out, Elsie Holland and the children were out walking and Megan had gone for a bicycle ride.

The letter must have come by the afternoon post. Mrs. Symmington must have taken it out of the box, read it—and then in a state of agitation she had gone to the potting shed, fetched some of the cyanide kept there for taking wasps' nests, dissolved it in water and drunk it after writing those last agitated words, "I can't go on . . ."

Owen Griffith gave medical evidence and stressed the view he had outlined to us of Mrs. Symmington's nervous condition and poor stamina. The coroner was suave and discreet. He spoke with bitter condemnation of people who write those despicable things, anonymous letters. Whoever had written that wicked and lying letter was morally guilty of murder, he said. He hoped the police would soon discover the culprit and take action against him or her. Such a dastardly and malicious piece of spite deserved to be punished with the utmost rigor of the law. Directed by him, the jury brought in the inevitable verdict: Suicide while temporarily insane.

The coroner had done his best—Owen Griffith also, but afterward, jammed in the crowd of eager village women, I heard the same hateful sibilant whisper I had begun to know so well: "No smoke without fire, that's what *I* say!" "Must 'a been something in it for certain sure. She wouldn't never have done it otherwise . . ."

Just for a moment I hated Lymstock and its

narrow boundaries, and its gossiping whispering women.

Outside, Aimée Griffith said with a sigh:

"Well, that's over. Bad luck on Dick Symmington, its all having to come out. I wonder whether he'd ever had any suspicion."

I was startled.

"But surely you heard him say most emphatically that there wasn't a word of truth in that lying letter?"

"Of course he said so. Quite right. A man's got to stick up for his wife. Dick would." She paused and then explained: "You see, I've known Dick Symmington a long time."

"Really?" I said surprised. "I understood from your brother that he only bought this practice a few years ago."

"Yes, but Dick Symmington used to come and stay in our part of the world up north. I've known him for years."

I looked at Aimée curiously. She went on, still in that softened tone, "I know Dick very well . . . He's a proud man and very reserved. But he's the sort of man who could be very jealous."

"That would explain," I said deliberately, "why Mrs. Symmington was afraid to show him or tell him about the letter. She was afraid that, being a jealous man, he might not believe her denials."

Miss Griffith looked at me angrily and scornfully. "Good Lord," she said. "Do you think any woman would go and swallow a lot of cyanide of potassium for an accusation that wasn't true?"

"The coroner seemed to think it was possible. Your brother, too—"

Aimée interrupted me:

"Men are all alike. All for preserving the decencies. But you don't catch *me* believing that stuff. If an innocent woman gets some foul anonymous letter, she laughs and chucks it away. That's what I—" she paused suddenly, and then finished—"would do."

But I had noticed the pause. I was almost sure that what she had been about to say was "That's what I did."

I decided to take the war into the enemy's country.

"I see," I said pleasantly. "So you've had one, too?"

Aimée Griffith was the type of woman who scorns to lie. She paused a minute—flushed, then said, "Well, yes. But I didn't let it worry me!"

"Nasty?" I inquired sympathetically, as a fellow sufferer.

"Naturally. These things always are. The ravings of a lunatic! I read a few words of it, realized what it was and chucked it straight into the wastepaper basket."

"You didn't think of taking it to the police?"

"Not then. Least said soonest mended—that's what I felt."

An urge came over me to say solemnly, "No smoke without fire!" but I restrained myself.

I asked her if she had any idea how her mother's death would affect Megan financially. Would it be necessary for the girl to earn her own living?

"I believe she has a small income left her by her grandmother and of course Dick would always give her a home. But it would be much better for her to do something—not just slack about the way she does."

"I should have said Megan is at the age when a

girl wants to enjoy herself—not to work.''

Aimée flushed and said sharply, "You're like all men—you dislike the idea of women competing. It is incredible to you that women should want a career. It was incredible to my parents. I was anxious to study for a doctor. They would not hear of paying the fees. But they paid them readily for Owen. Yet I should have made a better doctor than my brother.''

"I'm sorry about that," I said. "It was tough on you. If one wants to do a thing—"

She went on quickly.

"Oh, I've got over it now. I've plenty of will power. My life is busy and active. I'm one of the happiest people in Lymstock. Plenty to do. But I go up in arms against the silly old-fashioned prejudice that woman's place is always the home.''

"I'm sorry if I offended you," I said. I had had no idea that Aimée Griffith could be so vehement.

3

I met Symmington in the town later in the day.

"Is it quite all right for Megan to say on with us for a bit?" I asked. "It's company for Joanna—she's rather lonely sometimes with none of her own friends."

"Oh—er—Megan? Oh, yes, very good of you."

I took a dislike to Symmington then which I never quite overcame. He had so obviously forgotten all about Megan. I wouldn't have minded if he had actively disliked the girl—a man may sometimes be jealous of a first husband's child—but he didn't dislike her, he just hardly noticed her. He felt toward her much as a man who doesn't care much for dogs would feel about a dog in the house. You notice it when you fall over it and swear at it, and you give it a vague pat sometimes when it presents itself to be patted. Symmington's complete indifference to his stepdaughter annoyed me very much.

53

I said, "What are you planning to do with her?"

"With Megan?" He seemed rather startled. "Well, she'll go on living at home. I mean, naturally, it is her home."

My grandmother, of whom I had been very fond, used to sing old-fashioned songs to her guitar. One of them, I remember, ended thus:

"*Oh, maid most dear, I am not here,*
  I have no place, no part,
 No dwelling more, by sea nor shore,
  But only in your heart."

I went home humming it.

Emily Barton came just after tea had been cleared away.

She wanted to talk about the garden.

We talked garden for about half an hour. Then we turned back toward the house.

It was then that lowering her voice, she murmured, "I do hope that that child—that she hasn't been too much *upset* by all this dreadful business?"

"Her mother's death, you mean?"

"That, of course. But I really meant, the—the unpleasantness *behind* it."

I was curious. I wanted Miss Barton's reaction.

"What do you think about that? Was it true?"

"Oh, no, no, surely not. I'm quite sure that Mrs. Symmington never—that he wasn't—" little Emily Barton was pink and confused—"I mean it's quite untrue—although of course it may have been a judgment."

"A judgment?" I said, staring.

Emily Barton was very pink, very Dresden china shepherdesslike.

"I cannot help feeling that all these dreadful letters, all the sorrow and pain they have caused, may have been sent for a *purpose*."

"They were sent for a purpose, certainly," I said grimly.

"No, no, Mr. Burton, you misunderstand me. I'm not talking of the misguided creature who wrote them—someone quite abandoned that must be. I mean that they have been permitted—by Providence! To awaken us to a sense of our shortcomings."

"Surely," I said, "the Almighty could choose a less unsavory weapon."

Miss Emily murmured that God moved in a mysterious way.

"No," I said. "There's too much tendency to attribute to God the evils that man does of his own free will. I might concede you the Devil. God doesn't really need to punish us, Miss Barton. We're so very busy punishing ourselves."

"What I can't make out is *why* should anyone want to do such a thing?"

I shrugged my shoulders. "A warped mentality."

"It seems very sad."

"It doesn't seem to me sad. It seems to me just damnable. And I don't apologize for the word. I mean just that."

The pink had gone out of Miss Barton's cheeks. They were very white.

"But why, Mr. Burton, *why?* What pleasure can anyone get out of it?"

"Nothing you and I can understand, thank goodness."

Emily Barton lowered her voice; "Nothing of this kind has ever happened before—never in my memory. It has been such a happy little community. What would my dear mother have said? Well, one must be thankful that she has been spared."

I thought from all I heard that old Mrs. Barton had been sufficiently tough to have taken anything, and would probably have enjoyed this sensation.

Emily went on, "It distresses me deeply."

"You've not—er—had anything yourself?"

She flushed crimson. "Oh, no—oh, no, indeed. Oh! that would be dreadful."

I apologized hastily, but she went away looking rather upset.

I went into the house. Joanna was standing by the drawing-room fire which she had just lit, for the evenings were still chilly. She had an open letter in her hand.

She turned her head quickly as I entered.

"Jerry! I found this in the letter box—dropped in by hand. It begins: 'You painted trollop . . .' "

"What else does it say?"

Joanna gave a wide grimace. "Same old muck."

She dropped it on to the fire. With a quick gesture that hurt my back I jerked it off again just before it caught.

"Don't," I said. "We may need it."

"Need it?"

"For the police."

Superintendent Nash came to see me the following morning. From the first moment I saw him I took a great liking to him. He was the best type of C.I.D. County Superintendent. Tall, soldierly, with quiet, reflective eyes and a straightforward, unassuming manner.

"Good morning, Mr. Burton," he said. "I expect you can guess what I've come to see you about."

"Yes, I think so. This letter business."

He nodded.

"I understand you had one of them?"

"Yes, soon after we got here."

"What did it say exactly?"

I thought a minute, then conscientiously repeated the wording of the letter as closely as possible.

The superintendent listened with an immovable face, showing no signs of any kind of emotion.

When I had finished, he said, "I see. You didn't keep the letter, Mr. Burton?"

"I'm sorry. I didn't. You see, I thought it was just an isolated instance of spite against newcomers to the place."

The superintendent inclined his head comprehendingly.

"A pity," he said briefly.

"However," I said, "my sister got one yesterday. I just stopped her putting it in the fire."

"Thank you, Mr. Burton, that was thoughtful of you."

I went across to my desk and unlocked the drawer in which I had put it. It was not, I thought, very suitable for Partridge's eyes. I gave it to Nash.

He read it through. Then he looked up and asked:

"Is this the same in appearance as the last one?"

"I think so—as far as I can remember."

"The same difference between the envelope and the text?"

"Yes," I said. "The envelope was typed. The letter itself had printed words pasted on to a sheet of paper."

Nash nodded and put it in his pocket. Then he said:

"I wonder, Mr. Burton, if you would mind coming down to the station with me? We could have a conference there and it would save a good deal of time and overlapping."

"Certainly," I said. "You would like me to come now?"

"If you don't mind."

There was a police car at the door. We drove down in it.

I said, "Do you think you'll be able to get to the bottom of this?"

Nash nodded with easy confidence. "Oh, yes, we'll get to the bottom of it all right. It's a question of time and routine. They're slow, these cases, but they're pretty sure. It's a matter of narrowing things down."

"Elimination?" I said.

"Yes. And general routine."

"Watching post boxes, examining typewriters, fingerprints, all that?"

He smiled. "As you say."

At the police station I found Symmington and Griffith were already there. I was introduced to a tall, lantern-jawed man in plain clothes, Inspector Graves.

"Inspector Graves," explained Nash, "has come down from London to help us. He's an expert on anonymous letter cases."

Inspector Graves smiled mournfully. I reflected that a life spent in the pursuit of anonymous letter writers must be singularly depressing. Inspector Graves, however, showed a kind of melancholy enthusiasm.

"They're all the same, these cases," he said in a deep lugubrious voice like a depressed bloodhound. "You'd be surprised. The wording of the letters and the things they say."

"We had a case just on two years ago," said Nash. "Inspector Graves helped us then."

Some of the letters, I saw, were spread out on the table in front of Graves. He had evidently been examining them.

"Difficulty is," said Nash, "to get hold of the letters. Either people put them in the fire, or they won't admit to having received anything of the kind. Stupid, you see, and afraid of being mixed up with the police. They're a backward lot here."

"Still we've got a fair amount to get on with," said Graves. Nash took the letter I had given him from his pocket and tossed it over to Graves.

The latter glanced through it, laid it with the others and observed approvingly, "Very nice— very nice indeed."

It was not the way I should have chosen to describe the epistle in question, but experts, I suppose, have their own point of view. I was glad that that screed of vituperative and obscene abuse gave *somebody* pleasure.

"We've got enough, I think, to go on with," said Inspector Graves, "and I'll ask all you gentlemen, if you should get any more, to bring them along at once. Also, if you hear of someone else getting one (you, in particular, doctor, among your patients) do your best to get them to come along here with them. I've got"—he sorted with deft fingers among his exhibits—"one to Mr. Symmington, received as far back as two months ago, one to Dr. Griffith, one to Miss Ginch, one written to Mrs. Mudge, the butcher's wife, one to Jennifer Clark, barmaid at the Three Crowns, the one received by Mrs. Symmington, this one now to Miss Burton—oh, yes, and one to the bank manager."

"Quite a representative collection," I remarked.

"And not one I couldn't match from other cases! This one here is as near as nothing to one written by that milliner woman. This one is the dead spit of an outbreak we had up in Northumberland—written by a schoolgirl, they were. I can tell you, gentlemen, I'd like to see something *new* sometimes, instead of the same old treadmill."

"There is nothing new under the sun," I murmured.

"Quite so, sir. You'd know that if you were in our profession."

Nash sighed and said, "Yes, indeed."

Symmington asked, "Have you come to any definite opinion as to the writer?"

Graves cleared his throat and delivered a small lecture:

"There are certain similarities shared by all these letters. I shall enumerate them, gentlemen, in case they suggest anything to your minds. The text of the letters is composed of words made up from individual letters cut out of a printed book. It's an old book, printed, I should say, about the year 1830. This has obviously been done to avoid the risk of recognition through handwriting which is, as most people know nowadays, a fairly easy matter . . . the so-called disguising of a hand not amounting to much when faced with expert tests. There are no fingerprints on the letters and envelopes of a distinctive character. That is to say, they have been handled by the postal authorities, the recipient, and there are other stray fingerprints, but no set common to all, showing therefore that the person who put them together was careful to wear gloves.

"The envelopes are typewritten by a Windsor 7 machine, well worn, with the *a* and the *t* out of alignment. Most of them have been posted locally, or put in the box of a house by hand. It is therefore evident that they are of local provenance. They were written by a woman, and in my opinion a woman of middle age or over, and probably, though not certainly, unmarried."

We maintained a respectful silence for a minute or two. Then I said, "The typewriter's your best bet, isn't it? That oughtn't to be difficult in a little place like this."

Inspector Graves shook his head sadly and said, "That's where you're wrong, sir."

"The typewriter," said Superintendent Nash, "is unfortunately too easy. It is an old one from Mr. Symmington's office, given by him to the Women's Institute where, I may say, it's fairly easy of access. The ladies here all often go into the Institute."

"Can't you tell something definite from the—er—the touch, don't you call it?"

Again Graves nodded. "Yes, that can be done —but these envelopes have all been typed by someone using one finger."

"Someone, then, unused to the typewriter?"

"No, I wouldn't say that. Someone, perhaps, who can type but doesn't want us to know the fact."

"Whoever writes these things has been very cunning," I said slowly.

"She is, sir, she is," said Graves. "Up to every trick of the trade."

"I shouldn't have thought one of these bucolic women down here would have had the brains," I said.

Graves coughed. "I haven't made myself plain, I'm afraid. Those letters were written by an educated woman."

"What, by a lady?"

The word slipped out involuntarily. I hadn't used the term "lady" for years. But now it came automatically to my lips, re-echoed from days long ago, and my grandmother's faint unconsciously arrogant voice saying, "Of course, she isn't a *lady*, dear."

Nash understood at once. The word lady still meant something to him.

"Not necessarily a lady," he said. "But certainly not a village woman. They're mostly pretty illiterate down here, can't spell, and certainly can't express themselves with fluency."

I was silent, for I had had a shock. The community was so small. Unconsciously I had visualized the writer of the letters as a Mrs. Cleat or her like, some spiteful, cunning half-wit.

Symmington put my thoughts into words. He said sharply, "But that narrows it down to about half a dozen to a dozen people in the whole place! I can't believe it."

Then, with a slight effort, and looking straight in front of him as though the mere sound of his own words was distasteful, he said:

"You have heard what I stated at the inquest. In case you may have thought that that statement was actuated by a desire to protect my wife's memory, I should like to repeat now that I am firmly convinced that the subject matter of the letter my wife received was absolutely false. I *know* it was false. My wife was a very sensitive woman, and—er—well, you might call it *prudish* in some respects. Such a letter would have been a great shock to her, and she was in poor health."

Graves responded instantly:

"That's quite likely to be right, sir. None of these letters show any signs of intimate knowledge. They're just blind accusations. There's been no attempt to blackmail. And there doesn't seem to be any religious bias—such as we sometimes get. It's just sex and spite! And that's going to give us quite a good pointer toward the writer."

Symmington got up. Dry and unemotional as the man was, his lips were trembling.

"I hope you find the devil who writes these soon. She murdered my wife as surely as if she'd put a knife into her." He paused. "How does she feel now, I wonder?"

He went out, leaving that question unanswered.

"How does she feel, Griffith?" I asked. It seemed to me the answer was in his province.

"God knows. Remorseful, perhaps. On the other hand, it may be that she's enjoying her power. Mrs. Symmington's death may have fed her mania."

"I hope not," I said, with a slight shiver. "Because if so, she'll—"

I hesitated and Nash finished the sentence for me:

"She'll try it again? That, Mr. Burton, would be the best thing that could happen, for us. The pitcher goes to the well once too often, remember."

"She'd be mad to go on with it," I exclaimed.

"She'll go on," said Graves. "They always do. It's a vice, you know, they can't let it alone."

I shook my head with a shudder. I asked if they needed me any longer, I wanted to get out into the air. The atmosphere seemed tinged with evil.

"There's nothing more, Mr. Burton," said Nash. "Only keep your eyes open, and do as much propaganda as you can—that is to say, urge on everyone that they've got to report any letter they receive."

I nodded.

"I should think everyone in the place has had one of the foul things by now," I said.

"I wonder," said Graves. He put his sad head a little on one side and asked, "You don't know, definitely, of anyone who *hasn't* had a letter?"

"What an extraordinary question! The population at large isn't likely to take me into their confidence."

"No, no, Mr. Burton, I didn't mean that. I just wondered if you knew of any one person who quite definitely, to your certain knowledge, has not received an anonymous letter."

"Well, as a matter of fact," I hesitated, "I do, in a way."

And I repeated my conversation with Emily Barton and what she had said.

Graves received the information with a wooden face and said, "Well, that may come in useful. I'll note it down."

I went out into the afternoon sunshine with

Owen Griffith. Once in the street, I swore aloud.

"What kind of place is this for a man to come to to lie in the sun and heal his wounds? It's full of festering poison, this place, and it looks as peaceful and as innocent as the Garden of Eden."

"Even there," said Owen drily, "there was one serpent."

"Look here, Griffith, do they know anything? Have they got any idea?"

"I don't know. They've got a wonderful technique, the police. They're seemingly so frank, and they tell you nothing."

"Yes. Nash is a nice fellow."

"And a very capable one."

"If anyone's batty in this place, you ought to know it," I said accusingly.

Griffith shook his head. He looked discouraged. But he looked more than that—he looked worried. I wondered if he had an inkling of some kind.

We had been walking along the High Street. I stopped at the door of the house agents.

"I believe my second installment of rent is due—in advance. I've got a good mind to pay it and clear out with Joanna right away. Forfeit the rest of the tenancy."

"Don't go," said Owen.

"Why not?"

He didn't answer. He said slowly after a minute or two, "After all—I dare say you're right. Lymstock isn't healthy just now. It might—it might harm you or—or your sister."

"Nothing harms Joanna," I said. "She's tough. I'm the weakly one. Somehow this business makes me sick."

"It makes *me* sick," said Owen.

I pushed the door of the house agents' place half open.

"But I shan't go," I said. "Vulgar curiosity is stronger than pusillanimity. I want to know the solution."

I went in.

A woman who was typing got up and came toward me. She had frizzy hair and simpered, but I found her more intelligent than the spectacled youth who had previously held sway in the outer office.

A minute or two later something familiar about her penetrated through to my consciousness. It was Miss Ginch, lately Symmington's lady clerk.

I commented on the fact.

"You used to be with Galbraith, Galbraith and Symmington, weren't you?" I said.

"Yes. Yes, indeed. But I thought it was better to leave. This is quite a good post, though not quite so well paid. But there are things that are more valuable than money, don't you think so?"

"Undoubtedly," I said.

"Those awful letters," breathed Miss Ginch in a sibilant whisper. "I got a dreadful one. About me and Mr. Symmington—oh, terrible it was, saying the most *awful* things! I knew my duty and I look it to the police, though of course it wasn't exactly *pleasant* for me, was it?"

"No, no, most unpleasant."

"But they thanked me and said I had done quite right. But I felt that, after that, if people were talking—and evidently they *must* have been, or where did the writer get the idea from?—then I must avoid even the appearance of evil, though there has never been anything at all *wrong* between me and Mr. Symmington."

I felt rather embarrassed.

"No, no, of course not."

"But people have such evil minds. Yes, alas, such evil minds!"

Nervously trying to avoid it, I nevertheless met her eye, and I made a most unpleasant discovery.

Miss Ginch was thoroughly enjoying herself.

Already once today I had come across someone who reacted pleasurably to anonymous letters. Inspector Graves' enthusiasm was professional. Miss Ginch's enjoyment I found merely suggestive and disgusting.

An idea flashed across my startled mind.

Had Miss Ginch written these letters herself?

When I got home I found Mrs. Dane Calthrop sitting talking to Joanna. She looked, I thought, gray and ill.

"This has been a terrible shock to me, Mr. Burton," she said. "Poor thing, poor thing."

"Yes," I said. "It's awful to think of someone being driven to the stage of taking their own life."

"Oh, you mean Mrs. Symmington?"

"Didn't you?"

Mrs. Dane Calthrop shook her head. "Of course one is sorry for her, but it would have been bound to happen anyway, wouldn't it?"

"Would it?" said Joanna drily.

Mrs. Dane Calthrop turned to her.

"Oh, I think so, dear. If suicide is your idea of escape from trouble then it doesn't very much matter what the trouble is. Whenever some very unpleasant shock had to be faced, she'd have done the same thing. What it really comes down to is that she was that kind of woman. Not that one would have guessed it. She always seemed to me a selfish rather stupid woman, with a good firm hold on life. Not the kind to panic, you would think—but I'm beginning to realize how little I really know about anyone."

"I'm still curious as to whom you meant when you said 'Poor thing,' " I remarked.

She stared at me. "The woman who wrote the letters, of course."

"I don't think," I said drily, "I shall waste sympathy on her."

Mrs. Dane Calthrop leaned forward. She laid a hand on my knee.

"But don't you realize—can't you *feel?* Use your imagination. Think how desperately, violently unhappy anyone must be to sit down and write those things. How lonely, how cut off from human kind. Poisoned through and through, with a dark stream of poison that finds its outlet in this way. That's why I feel so self-reproachful. Somebody in this town has been racked with that terrible unhappiness, and I've had no idea of it. I should have had. You can't interfere with actions —I never do. But that black inward unhappiness —like a septic arm physically, all black and swollen. If you could cut it and let the poison out it would flow away harmlessly. Yes, poor soul, poor soul."

She got up to go.

I did not feel like agreeing with her. I had no sympathy for our anonymous letter writer whatsoever. But I did ask curiously:

"Have you any idea at all, Mrs. Calthrop, who this woman is?"

She turned her fine perplexed eyes on me. "Well, I can guess," she said. "But then I might be wrong, mightn't I?"

She went swiftly out through the door, popping her head back to ask: "Do tell me, why have you never married, Mr. Burton?"

In anyone else it would have been impertinence, but with Mrs. Dane Calthrop you felt that the idea had suddenly come into her head and she had really wanted to know.

"Shall we say," I said, rallying, "that I have never met the right woman?"

"We can say so," said Mrs. Dane Calthrop, "but it wouldn't be a very good answer, because so many men have obviously married the wrong woman."

This time she really departed.

Joanna said, "You know I really do think she's mad. But I like her. The people in the village here are afraid of her."

"So am I, a little."

"Because you never know what's coming next?"

"Yes. And there's a careless brilliancy about her guesses."

Joanna said slowly, "Do you really think whoever wrote these letters is very unhappy?"

"I don't know what the damned hag is thinking or feeling! And I don't care. It's her victims I'm sorry for."

It seems odd to me now that in our speculations about Poison Pen's frame of mind, we missed the most obvious one. Griffith had pictured her as possibly exultant. I had envisaged her as remorseful—appalled by the result of her handiwork. Mrs. Dane Calthrop had seen her as suffering.

Yet the obvious, the inevitable reaction we did not consider—or perhaps I should say, I did not consider. That reaction was Fear.

For with the death of Mrs. Symmington, the letters had passed out of one category into another. I don't know what the legal position was—Symmington knew, I suppose, but it was clear that with a death resulting, the position of the writer of the letters was much more serious. There could now be no question of passing it off as a joke if the identity of the writer was discovered. The police were active, a Scotland Yard expert was called in. It was vital now for the anonymous author to remain anonymous.

And granted that Fear was the principal reaction, other things followed. Those possibilities also I was blind to. Yet surely they should have been obvious.

Joanna and I came down rather late to breakfast the next morning. That is to say, late by the standards of Lymstock. It was nine-thirty, an hour at which, in London, Joanna was just unclosing an eyelid, and mine would probably be still tight shut.

However when Partridge had said, "Breakfast at half past eight, or nine o'clock?" neither Joanna nor I had had the nerve to suggest a later hour.

To my annoyance, Aimée Griffith was standing on the doorstep talking to Megan.

She gave tongue with her usual heartiness at the sight of us:

"Hullo, there, slackers! I've been up for hours."

That, of course, was her own business. A doctor, no doubt, has to have early breakfast, and a dutiful sister is there to pour out his tea or coffee. But it is no excuse for coming and butting in on one's more somnolent neighbors. Nine-thirty is not the time for a morning call.

Megan slipped back into the house and into the dining room, where I gathered she had been interrupted in her breakfast.

"I said I wouldn't come in," said Aimée Griffith—"though why it is more of a merit to force people to come and speak to you on the doorstep, than to talk to them inside the house I do not know. Just wanted to ask Miss Burton if she'd any vegetables to spare for our Red Cross stall on the main road. If so, I'd get Owen to call for them in the car."

"You're out and about very early," I said.

"The early bird catches the worm," said Aimée. "You have a better chance of finding people in this time of day. I'm off to Mr. Pye's next. Got to go over to Brenton this afternoon. Guides."

"Your energy makes me quite tired," I said, and at that moment the telephone rang and I retired to the back of the hall to answer it, leaving Joanna murmuring rather doubtfully something about rhubarb and French beans and exposing her ignorance of the vegetable garden.

"Yes?" I said into the telephone mouthpiece.

A confused noise of deep breathing came from the other end of the wire and a doubtful female voice said, "Oh!"

"Yes?" I said again encouragingly.

"Oh," said the voice again, and then it inquired adenoidally, "Is that—what I mean—is that Little Furze?"

"This is Little Furze."

"Oh!" This clearly a stock beginning to every sentence. The voice inquired cautiously: "Could I speak to Miss Partridge just a minute?"

"Certainly," I said. "Who shall I say?"

"Oh. Tell her it's Agnes, would you? Agnes Waddle."

"Agnes Waddle?"

"That's right."

Resisting the temptation to say "Donald Duck to you," I put down the telephone receiver and called up the stairs to where I could hear the sound of Partridge's activities overhead.

"Partridge! Partridge!"

Partridge appeared at the head of the stairs, a long mop in one hand, and a look of "What is it *now?*" clearly discernible behind her invariably respectful manner.

"Yes, sir?"

"Agnes Waddle wants to speak to you on the telephone."

"I beg your pardon, sir?"

I raised my voice: "Agnes Waddle."

I have spelled the name as it presented itself to my mind. But I will now spell it as it was actually written:

"Agnes Woddell—whatever can she want now?"

Very much put out of countenance Partridge relinquished her mop and rustled down the stairs, her print dress crackling with agitation.

I beat an unobtrusive retreat into the dining room where Megan was wolfing down kidneys and bacon. Megan, unlike Aimée Griffith, was displaying no "glorious morning face." In fact she replied very gruffly to my morning salutations and continued to eat in silence.

I opened the morning paper and a minute or two later Joanna entered looking somewhat shattered.

"Whew!" she said. "I'm so tired. And I think I've exposed my utter ignorance of what grows when. Aren't there runner beans this time of year?"

"August," said Megan.

"Well, one has them any time in London," said Joanna defensively.

"Tins, sweet fool," I said. "And cold storage on ships from the far-flung limits of Empire."

"Like ivory, apes and peacocks?" asked Joanna.

"Exactly."

"I'd rather have peacocks," said Joanna thoughtfully.

"I'd like a monkey of my own as a pet," said Megan.

Meditatively peeling an orange, Joanna said:

"I wonder what it would feel like to be Aimée Griffith, all bursting with health and vigor and enjoyment of life. Do you think she's ever tired, or depressed, or—or wistful?"

I said I was quite certain Aimée Griffith was never wistful, and followed Megan out of the open French window onto the veranda.

Standing there, filling my pipe, I heard Partridge enter the dining room from the hall and heard her voice say grimly, "Can I speak to you a minute, Miss?"

"Dear me," I thought. "I hope Partridge isn't going to give notice. Emily Barton would be very annoyed with us if so."

Partridge went on:

"I must apologize, Miss, for being rung up on the telephone. That is to say, the young person who did so should have known better. I have never been in the habit of using the telephone or of per-

mitting my friends to ring me up on it, and I'm
very sorry indeed that it should have occurred,
and the master taking the call and everything."

"Why, that's quite all right, Partridge," said
Joanna soothingly, "why shouldn't your friends
use the phone if they want to speak to you?"

Partridge's face, I could feel, though I could
not see it, was more dour than ever as she replied
coldly:

"It is not the kind of thing that has ever been
done in this house. Miss Emily would never permit
it. As I say, I am sorry it occurred, but Agnes
Woddell, the girl who did it, was upset and she's
young too, and doesn't know what's fitting in a
gentleman's house."

"That's one for you, Joanna," I thought
gleefully.

"This Agnes who rung me up, Miss," went on
Partridge, "she used to be in service here under
me. Sixteen she was, then, and come straight from
the orphanage. And you see, not having a home,
or a mother or any relations to advise her, she's
been in the habit of coming to me. I can tell her
what's what, you see."

"Yes?" said Joanna and waited. Clearly there
was more to follow.

"So I am taking the liberty of asking you, Miss,
if you would allow Agnes to come here to tea this
afternoon in the kitchen. It's her day out, you see,
and she's got something on her mind she wants to
consult me about. I wouldn't dream of suggesting
such a thing in the usual way."

Joanna said bewildered, "But why shouldn't
you have anyone to tea with you?"

Partridge drew herself up at this, so Joanna said

afterward and really looked most formidable, as she replied:

"It has never been the custom of this house, Miss. Old Mrs. Barton never allowed visitors in the kitchen, excepting as it should be our own day out, in which case we were allowed to entertain friends here instead of going out, but otherwise, on ordinary days, no. And Miss Emily keeps to the old ways."

Joanna is very nice to servants and most of them like her but she has never cut any ice with Partridge.

"It's no good, my girl," I said when Partridge had gone and Joanna had joined me outside. "Your sympathy and leniency are not appreciated. The good old overbearing ways for Partridge and things done the way they should be done in a gentleman's house."

"I never heard of such tyranny as not allowing them to have their friends to see them," said Joanna. "It's all very well, Jerry, but they can't *like* being treated like black slaves."

"Evidently they do," I said. "At least the Partridges of this world do."

"I can't imagine why she doesn't like me. Most people do."

"She probably despises you as an inadequate housekeeper. You never draw your hand across a shelf and examine it for traces of dust. You don't look under the mats. You don't ask what happened to the remains of the chocolate soufflé, and you never order a nice bread pudding."

"Ugh!" said Joanna.

She went on sadly: "I'm a failure all around to-day. Despised by our Aimée for ignorance of the vegetable kingdom. Snubbed by Partridge for being a human being. I shall now go out into the garden and eat worms.''

''Megan's there already,'' I said.

For Megan had wandered away a few minutes previously and was now standing aimlessly in the middle of a patch of lawn looking not unlike a meditative bird waiting for nourishment.

She came back however toward us and said abruptly, ''I say, I must go home today.''

''What?'' I was dismayed.

She went on, flushing, but speaking with nervous determination:

''It's been awfully good of you having me and I expect I've been a fearful nuisance, but I have enjoyed it awfully, only now I must go back, because after all, well, it's my home and one can't stay away for ever, so I think I'll go this morning.''

Both Joanna and I tried to make her change her mind, but she was quite adamant, and finally Joanna got out the car and Megan went upstairs and came down a few minutes later with her belongings packed up again.

The only person pleased seemed to be Partridge, who had almost a smile on her grim face. She had never liked Megan much.

I was standing in the middle of the lawn when Joanna returned.

She asked me if I thought I was a sundial.

''Why?''

''Standing there like a garden ornament. Only one couldn't put on you the motto of only marking the sunny hours. You looked like thunder!''

''I'm out of humor. First Aimée Griffith— 'Gracious!' murmured Joanna in parenthesis, 'I must speak about those vegetables!' and then

Megan beetling off. I'd thought of taking her for a walk up to Legge Tor."

"With a collar and lead, I suppose," said Joanna.

"What?"

Joanna repeated loudly and clearly as she moved off around the corner of the house to the kitchen garden:

"I said 'With a collar and lead, I suppose?' Master's lost his dog, that's what's the matter with you!"

4

I was annoyed, I must confess, at the abrupt way
in which Megan had left us. Perhaps she had suddenly got bored with us.

After all, it wasn't a very amusing life for a girl.
At home she had the kids and Elsie Holland.

I heard Joanna returning and hastily moved in
case she should make more rude remarks about
sundials.

Owen Griffith called in his car just before lunch
time, and the gardener was waiting for him with
the necessary garden produce.

While Old Adams was stowing it in the car I
brought Owen indoors for a drink. He wouldn't
stay to lunch.

When I came in with the sherry I found Joanna
had begun doing her stuff.

No signs of animosity now. She was curled up in
the corner of the sofa and was positively purring,
asking Owen questions about his work, if he liked

79

being a G. P., if he wouldn't rather have special-
ized? She thought doctoring was one of the most
fascinating things in the world.

Say what you will of her, Joanna is a lovely, a
heaven-born listener. And after listening to so
many would-be geniuses telling her how they had
been unappreciated, listening to Owen Griffith
was easy money. By the time we had got to the
third glass of sherry, Griffith was telling her about
some obscure reaction or lesion in such scientific
terms that nobody could have understood a word
of it except a fellow medico.

Joanna was looking intelligent and deeply interested.

I felt a moment's qualm. It was really too bad
of Joanna. Griffith was too good a chap to be
played fast and loose with. Women really were
devils.

Then I caught a sideways view of Griffith, his
long, purposeful chin and the grim set of his lips,
and I was not so sure that Joanna was going to
have it her own way after all. And anyway a man
has no business to let himself be made a fool of by
a woman. It's his own lookout if he does.

Then Joanna said:

"Do change your mind and stay to lunch with
us, Dr. Griffith," and Griffith flushed a little and
said he would, only his sister would be expecting
him back—

"We'll ring her up and explain," said Joanna
quickly and went out into the hall and did so.

I thought Griffith looked a little uneasy, and it
crossed my mind that he was probably a little
afraid of his sister.

Joanna came back smiling and said that that
was all right.

And Owen Griffith stayed to lunch and seemed to enjoy himself. We talked about books and plays and world politics, and about music and painting and modern architecture.

We didn't talk about Lymstock at all, or about anonymous letters, or Mrs. Symmington's suicide.

We got right away from everything, and I think Owen Griffith was happy. His dark sad face lighted up, and he revealed an interesting mind.

When he had gone I said to Joanna, "That fellow's too good for your tricks."

"That's what *you* say!" Joanna said. "You men all stick together!"

"Why are you out after his hide, Joanna? Wounded vanity?"

"Perhaps," said my sister.

That afternoon we were to go to tea with Miss Emily Barton at her rooms in the village.

We strolled down there on foot, for I felt strong enough now to manage the hill back again.

We must actually have allowed too much time and got there early, for the door was opened to us by a tall, raw-boned, fierce-looking woman who told us that Miss Barton wasn't in yet.

"But she's expecting you, I know, so if you'll come up and wait, please."

This was evidently faithful Florence.

We followed her up the stairs and she threw open a door and showed us into what was quite a comfortable sitting room, though perhaps a little over-furnished. Some of the things, I suspected, had come from Little Furze.

The woman was clearly proud of her room.

"It's nice, isn't it?" she demanded.

"Very nice," said Joanna warmly.

"I make her as comfortable as I can. Not that I can do for her as I'd like to and in the way she ought to have. She ought to be in her own house, properly, not turned out into rooms."

Florence, who was clearly a dragon, looked from one to the other of us reproachfully. It was not, I felt, our lucky day. Joanna had been ticked off by Aimée Griffith and Partridge and now we were both being ticked off by the dragon Florence.

"Parlormaid I was for nine years there," she added.

Joanna, goaded by injustice, said, "Well, Miss Barton wanted to let the house. She put it down at the house agents."

"Forced to it," said Florence. "And she living so frugal and careful. But even then, the government can't leave her alone! Has to have its pound of flesh just the same."

I shook my head sadly.

"Plenty of money there was in the old lady's time," said Florence. "And then they all died off one after another, poor dears. Miss Emily nursing of them one after the other. Wore herself out she did, and always so patient and uncomplaining. But it told on her, and then to have worry about money on top of it all! Shares not bringing in what they used to, so she says, and why not, I should like to know? They ought to be ashamed of themselves. Doing down a lady like her who's got no head for figures and can't be up to their tricks."

"Practically everyone has been hit that way," I said, but Florence remained unsoftened.

"It's all right for some as can look after themselves, but not for *her*. She needs looking after, and as long as she's with me I'm going to see no one imposes on her or upsets her in any way. I'd do anything for Miss Emily.''

And glaring at us for some moments in order to drive that point thoroughly home, the indomitable Florence left the room, carefully shutting the door behind her.

"Do you feel like a bloodsucker, Jerry?" inquired Joanna. "Because I do. What's the matter with us?''

"We don't seem to be going down very well," I said. "Megan gets tired of us, Partridge disapproves of you, faithful Florence disapproves of both of us.''

Joanna murmured, "I wonder why Megan *did* leave?''

"She got bored.''

"I don't think she did at all. I wonder—do you think, Jerry, it could have been something that Aimée Griffith said?''

"You mean this morning, when they were talking on the doorstep?''

"Yes. There wasn't much time, of course, but—''

I finished the sentence: "But that woman's got the tread of a cow elephant! She might have—''

The door opened and Miss Emily came in. She was pink and a little out of breath and seemed excited. Her eyes were very blue and shining.

She chirruped at us in quite a distracted manner:

"Oh, dear, I'm so sorry I'm late. Just doing a little shopping in the town, and the cakes at the Blue Rose didn't seem to me quite fresh, so I went on to Mrs. Lygon's. I always like to get my cakes the last thing, then one gets the newest batch just out of the oven, and one isn't put off with the day before's. But I am so distressed to have kept you waiting—really unpardonable—"

Joanna cut in:

"It's our fault, Miss Barton. We're early. We walked down and Jerry strides along so fast now that we arrive everywhere too soon."

"Never too soon, dear. Don't say that. One cannot have too much of a good thing, you know."

And the old lady petted Joanna affectionately on the shoulder.

Joanna brightened up. At last, so it seemed, she was being a success. Emily Barton extended her smile to include me, but with a slight timidity in it, rather as one might approach a man-eating tiger guaranteed for the moment harmless.

"It's very good of you to come to such a feminine meal as tea, Mr. Burton."

Emily Barton, I think, has a mental picture of men as interminably consuming whisky-and-sodas and smoking cigars, and in the intervals dropping out to do a few seductions of village maidens, or to conduct a liaison with a married woman.

When I said this to Joanna later, she replied that it was probably wishful thinking, that Emily Barton would have liked to come across such a man, but alas, had never done so.

In the meantime, Miss Emily was fussing around the room, arranging Joanna and myself with little tables, and carefully providing ashtrays, and a minute later the door opened and Florence came in bearing a tray of tea with some fine Crown Derby cups on it, which I gathered Miss Emily had brought with her. The tea was China and delicious and there were plates of sandwiches and thin bread and butter, and a quantity of little cakes.

Florence was beaming now, and looked at Miss Emily with a kind of maternal pleasure, as at a favorite child enjoying a doll's tea party.

Joanna and I ate far more than we wanted to, our hostess pressed us so earnestly. The little lady was clearly enjoying her tea party and I perceived that to Emily Barton, Joanna and I were a big adventure, two people from the mysterious world of London and sophistication.

Naturally, our talk soon dropped into local channels. Miss Barton spoke warmly of Dr. Griffith, his kindness and his cleverness as a doctor. Mr. Symmington, too, was a very clever lawyer, and had helped Miss Barton to get some money back from the Income Tax which she would never have known about. He was so nice to his children, too, devoted to them and to his wife—she caught herself up. "Poor Mrs. Symmington, it's so dreadfully sad, with those young children left motherless. Never, perhaps, a very strong woman —and her health had been bad of late.

"A brain storm, that is what it must have been. I read about such a thing in the paper. People really do not know what they are doing under those circumstances. And she can't have known what she was doing or else she would have remembered Mr. Symmington and the children."

"That anonymous letter must have shaken her up very badly," said Joanna.

Miss Barton flushed. She said, with a tinge of reproof in her voice:

"Not a very nice thing to discuss, do you think,

dear? I know there have been—er—letters, but we won't talk about them. Nasty things. I think they are better just ignored."

Well, Miss Barton might be able to ignore them, but for some people it wasn't so easy. However I obediently changed the subject and we discussed Aimée Griffith.

"Wonderful, quite wonderful," said Emily Barton. "Her energy and her organizing powers are really splendid. She's so good with girls too. And she's so practical and up to date in every way. She really runs this place. And absolutely devoted to her brother. It's very nice to see such devotion between brother and sister."

"Doesn't he ever find her a little overwhelming?" asked Joanna.

Emily Barton stared at her in a startled fashion.

"She has sacrificed a great deal for his sake," she said with a touch of reproachful dignity.

I saw a touch of Oh, Yeah? in Joanna's eye and hastened to divert the conversation to Mr. Pye.

Emily Barton was a little dubious about Mr. Pye.

All she could say was, repeated rather doubtfully, that he was very kind—yes, very kind. Very well off, too, and most generous. He had very strange visitors sometimes, but then, of course, he had traveled a lot.

We agreed that travel not only broadened the mind, but occasionally resulted in the forming of strange acquaintances.

"I have often wished, myself, to go on a cruise," said Emily Barton wistfully. "One reads about them in the papers and they sound so attractive."

"Why don't you go?" asked Joanna.

This turning of a dream into a reality seemed to alarm Miss Emily.

"Oh, no, no, that would be *quite* impossible."

"But why? They're fairly cheap."

"Oh, it's not only the expense. But I shouldn't like to go alone. Traveling alone would look very peculiar, don't you think?"

"No," said Joanna.

Miss Emily looked at her doubtfully.

"And I don't know how I would manage about my luggage—and going ashore at foreign ports—and all the different currencies—"

Innumerable pitfalls seemed to rise up before the little lady's affrighted gaze, and Joanna hastened to calm her by a question about an approaching garden fete and sale of work. This led us quite naturally to Mrs. Dane Calthrop.

A faint spasm showed for a minute on Miss Barton's face. "You know, dear," she said, "she is really a very *odd* woman. The things she says sometimes."

I asked what things.

"Oh, I don't know. Such very *unexpected* things. And the way she looks at you, as though you weren't there but somebody else was—I'm expressing it badly but it is so hard to convey the impression I mean. And then she won't—well, *interfere* at all. There are so many cases where a vicar's wife could advise and—perhaps *admonish*. Pull people up, you know, and make them mend their ways. Because people would listen to her, I'm sure of that, they're all quite in awe of her. But she insists on being aloof and far away, and has such a curious habit of feeling sorry for the most unworthy people."

"That's interesting," I said, exchanging a quick glance with Joanna.

"Still, she is a very well-bred woman. She was a Miss Farroway of Bellpath, very good family, but these old families sometimes *are* a little peculiar, I believe. But she is devoted to her husband who is a man of very fine intellect—wasted, I am sometimes afraid, in this country circle. A good man, and most sincere, but I always find his habit of quoting Latin a little confusing."

"Hear, hear," I said fervently.

"Jerry had an expensive public school education, so he doesn't recognize Latin when he hears it," said Joanna.

This led Miss Barton to a new topic.

"The schoolmistress here is a most unpleasant young woman," she said. "Quite *Red*, I'm afraid." She lowered her voice over the word "Red."

Later, as we walked home up the hill, Joanna said to me:

"She's rather sweet."

At dinner that night Joanna said to Partridge that she hoped her tea party had been a success.

Partridge got rather red in the face and held herself even more stiffly. "Thank you, Miss, but Agnes never turned up after all."

"Oh, I'm sorry."

"It didn't matter to *me*," said Partridge.

She was so swelling with grievance that she condescended to pour it out to us:

"It wasn't me who thought of asking her! She rang up herself, said she'd something on her mind

and could she come here, it being her day off. And
I said, yes, subject to your permission which I ob-
tained. And after that, not a sound or sign of her!
And no word of apology either, though I should
hope I'll get a postcard tomorrow morning. These
girls nowadays—don't know their place—no idea
of how to behave."

Joanna attempted to soothe Partridge's
wounded feelings:

"She mightn't have felt well. You didn't ring up
to find out?"

Partridge drew herself up again. "No, I did *not*,
Miss! No, indeed. If Agnes likes to behave rudely
that's her lookout, but I shall give her a piece of
my mind when we meet."

Partridge went out of the room still stiff with
indignation, and Joanna and I laughed.

"Probably a case of 'Advice from Aunt
Nancy's Column,' " I said. " '*My boy is very
cold in his manner to me, what shall I do about
it?*' Failing Aunt Nancy, Partridge was to be ap-
plied to for advice, but instead there has been a
reconciliation and I expect at this minute that
Agnes and her boy are one of those speechless
couples locked in each other's arms that you come
upon suddenly standing by a dark hedge. They
embarrass you horribly, but you don't embarrass
them."

Joanna laughed and said she expected that was
it.

We began talking of the anonymous letters and
wondered how Nash and the melancholy Graves
were getting on.

"It's a week today exactly," said Joanna,
"since Mrs. Symmington's suicide. I should think

they must have got on to something by now. Fingerprints, or handwriting, or *something.*"

I answered her absently. Somewhere behind my conscious mind, a queer uneasiness was growing. It was connected in some way with the phrase that Joanna had used, "a week exactly."

I ought, I dare say, to have put two and two together earlier. Perhaps, unconsciously, my mind was already suspicious.

Anyway the leaven was working now. The uneasiness was growing—coming to a head.

Joanna noticed suddenly that I wasn't listening to her spirited account of a village encounter.

"What's the matter, Jerry?"

I did not answer because my mind was busy piecing things together.

Mrs. Symmington's suicide. . . . She was alone in the house that afternoon. . . . Alone in the house *because the maids were having their day out.* . . . A week ago exactly. . . .

"Jerry, what—"

I interrupted:

"Joanna, maids have days out once a week, don't they?"

"And alternate Sundays," said Joanna. "What on—"

"Never mind Sundays. They go out the same day every week?"

"Yes. That's the usual thing."

Joanna was staring at me curiously. Her mind had not taken the track mine had.

I crossed the room and rang the bell.

Partridge came.

"Tell me," I said, "this Agnes Woddell. She's in service?"

"Yes, sir. At Mrs. Symmington's. At Mr. Symmington's I should say now."

I drew a deep breath. I glanced at the clock. It was half past ten.

"Would she be back now, do you think?"

Partridge was looking disapproving. "Yes, sir. The maids have to be in by ten there. They're old-fashioned."

I said, "I'm going to ring up."

I went out to the hall. Joanna and Partridge followed me. Partridge was clearly furious. Joanna was puzzled. She said as I was trying to get the number, "What are you going to do, Jerry?"

"I'd like to be sure that the girl has come in all right."

Partridge sniffed. Just sniffed, nothing more. But I did not care twopence about Partridge's sniffs.

Elsie Holland answered the telephone from the other end.

"Sorry to ring you up," I said. "This is Jerry Burton speaking. Is—has—your maid Agnes come in?"

It was not until after I had said it that I suddenly felt a bit of a fool. For if the girl had come in and it was all right, how on earth was I going to explain my ringing up and asking. It would have been better if I had let Joanna ask the question, though even that would need a bit of explaining. I foresaw a new trail of gossip started in Lymstock, with myself and the unknown Agnes Woddell as its center.

Elsie Holland sounded, not unnaturally, very much surprised: "Agnes? Oh, she's sure to be in by now."

I felt a fool, but I went on with it: "Do you mind just seeing if she has come in, Miss Holland?"

There is one thing to be said for a nursery governess; she is used to doing things when told. Hers not to reason why! Elsie Holland put down the receiver and went off obediently.

Two minutes later I heard her voice:

"Are you there, Mr. Burton?"

"Yes."

"Agnes isn't in yet, as a matter of fact."

I knew then that my hunch had been right.

I heard a noise of voices vaguely from the other end, then Symmington himself spoke:

"Hullo, Burton, what's the matter?"

"Your maid Agnes isn't back yet."

"No. Miss Holland has just been to see. What's the matter? There's not been an accident, has there?"

"Not an *accident*," I said.

"Do you mean you have reason to believe something has happened to the girl?"

I said grimly, "I shouldn't be surprised."

I slept badly that night.

I think that, even then, there were pieces of the puzzle floating about in my mind. I believe that if I had given my mind to it, I could have solved the whole thing then and there. Otherwise why did those fragments tag along so persistently?

How much do we know at any time? Much more, or so I believe, than we know we know! But we cannot break through to that subterranean knowledge. It is there, but we cannot reach it.

I lay on my bed, tossing uneasily, and only vague bits of the puzzle came to torture me.

There was a pattern, if only I could get hold of it. I ought to know who wrote those damned letters. There was a trail somewhere if only I could follow it. . . .

As I dropped off to sleep, words danced irritatingly through my drowsy mind:

"No smoke without fire. No fire without smoke. Smoke. . . . Smoke? Smoke screen. . . . No, that was the war—a war phrase. War. Scrap of paper. . . . Only a scrap of paper. Belgium—Germany. . . ."

I fell asleep. I dreamed that I was taking Mrs. Dane Calthrop, who had turned into a greyhound, for a walk with a collar and lead.

It was the ringing of the telephone that roused me. A persistent ringing.

I sat up in bed, glanced at my watch. It was half past seven. I had not yet been called. The telephone was ringing in the hall downstairs.

I jumped out of bed, pulled on a dressing gown, and raced down. I beat Partridge coming through the back door from the kitchen by a short head. I picked up the receiver.

"Hullo?"

"Oh—" It was a sob of relief. "It's *you!*" Megan's voice. Megan's voice indescribably forlorn and frightened. "Oh, please do come—*do* come. Oh, please do! Will you?"

"I'm coming at once," I said. "Do you hear? *At once.*"

I took the stairs two at a time and burst in on Joanna.

"Look here, Jo, I'm going off to the Symmingtons'."

Joanna lifted a curly blond head from the pillow and rubbed her eyes like a small child.

"Why—what's happened?"

"I don't know. It was the child—Megan. She sounded all in."

"What do you think it is?"

"The girl Agnes, unless I'm very much mistaken."

As I went out of the door, Joanna called after me, "Wait. I'll get up and drive you down."

"No need. I'll drive myself."

"You can't drive the car."

"Yes, I can."

I did, too. It hurt, but not too much. I'd washed, shaved, dressed, got the car out and driven to the Symmingtons' in half an hour. Not bad going.

Megan must have been watching for me. She came out of the house at a run and clutched me. Her poor little face was white and twitching.

"Oh, you've come—you've *come!*"

"Hold up, funnyface," I said. "Yes, I've come. Now what is it?"

She began to shake. I put my arm around her.

"I—I found her."

"You found Agnes? Where?"

The trembling grew.

"Under the stairs. There's a cupboard there. It has fishing rods and golf clubs and things. You know."

I nodded. It was the usual cupboard.

Megan went on:

"She was there—all huddled up—and—and *cold*—horribly cold. She was—she was *dead,* you know!"

I asked curiously. "What made you look there?"

"I—I don't know. You telephoned last night. And we all began wondering where Agnes was. We waited up some time, but she didn't come in, and at last we went to bed. I didn't sleep very well and I got up early. There was only Rose (the cook, you know) about. She was very cross about Agnes not having come back. She said she'd been before somewhere when a girl did a flit like that. I had some milk and bread and butter in the kitchen— and then suddenly Rose came in looking queer and she said that Agnes' outdoor things were still in her room. Her best ones that she goes out in. And I began to wonder if—if she'd ever left the house, and I started looking around, and I opened the cupboard under the stairs and—and she was there . . ."

"Somebody's rung up the police, I suppose?"

"Yes, they're here now. My stepfather rang them up straightaway. And then I—I felt I couldn't bear it, and I rang *you* up. You don't mind?"

"No," I said. "I don't mind."

I looked at her curiously.

"Did anybody give you some brandy, or some coffee, or some tea after—after you found her?"

Megan shook her head.

I cursed the whole Symmington *ménage*. That stuffed shirt, Symmington, thought of nothing but the police. Neither Elsie Holland nor the cook seemed to have thought of the effect on the sensitive child who had made that gruesome discovery.

"Come on, slabface," I said. "We'll go to the kitchen."

We went around the house to the back door and into the kitchen. Rose, a plump pudding-faced woman of forty, was drinking strong tea by the kitchen fire. She greeted us with a flow of talk and her hand to her heart.

She'd come all over queer, she told me, awful the palpitations were! Just think of it, it might have been *her*, it might have been any of them, murdered in their beds they might have been.

"Dish out a good strong cup of that tea for Miss Megan," I said. "She's had a shock, you know. Remember it was she who found the body."

The mere mention of a body nearly sent Rose off again, but I quelled her with a stern eye and she poured out a cup of inky fluid.

"There you are, young woman," I said to Megan. "You drink that down. You haven't got any brandy, I suppose, Rose?"

Rose said rather doubtfully that there was a drop of cooking brandy left over from the Xmas puddings.

"That'll do," I said, and put a dollop of it into Megan's cup. I saw by Rose's eyes that she thought it a good idea.

I told Megan to stay with Rose.

"I can trust you to look after Miss Megan?" I said, and Rose replied in a gratified way, "Oh, yes, sir."

I went through into the house. If I knew Rose and her kind, she would soon find it necessary to keep her strength up with a little food, and that would be good for Megan too. Confound these people, why couldn't they look after the child?

Fuming inwardly I ran into Elsie Holland in the hall. She didn't seem surprised to see me. I suppose that the gruesome excitement of the discovery made one oblivious of who was coming and going. The constable, Bert Rundle, was by the front door.

Elsie Holland gasped out, "Oh, Mr. Burton, isn't it *awful?* Whoever can have done such a dreadful thing?"

"It was murder, then?"

"Oh, yes. She was struck on the back of the head. It's all blood and hair—oh! it's *awful*—and bundled into that cupboard. Who can have done such a wicked thing? And *why?* Poor Agnes, I'm sure she never did anyone any harm."

"No," I said. "Somebody saw to that pretty promptly."

She stared at me. Not, I thought, a quick-witted girl. But she had good nerves. Her color was as usual, slightly heightened by excitement, and I even fancied that in a macabre kind of way, and in spite of a naturally kind heart, she was enjoying the drama.

She said apologetically, "I must go up to the boys. Mr. Symmington is so anxious that they shouldn't get a shock. He wants me to keep them right away."

"Megan found the body, I hear," I said. "I hope somebody is looking after her."

I will say for Elsie Holland that she looked conscience-stricken.

"Oh, dear," she said. "I forgot all about her. I do hope she's all right. I've been so rushed, you know, and the police and everything—but it was remiss of me. Poor girl, she must be feeling bad. I'll go and look for her at once."

I relented.

"She's all right," I said. "Rose is looking after her. You get along to the kids."

She thanked me with a flash of white tombstone teeth and hurried upstairs. After all, the boys were her job, and not Megan—Megan was nobody's job. Elsie was paid to look after Symmington's blinking brats. One could hardly blame her for attending to it.

As she flashed around the corner of the stairs, I caught my breath. For a minute I caught a glimpse of a Winged Victory, deathless and incredibly beautiful, instead of a conscientious nursery governess.

Then a door opened and Superintendent Nash stepped out into the hall with Symmington behind him.

"Oh, Mr. Burton," he said, "I was just going to telephone you. I'm glad you are here."

He didn't ask me—then—why I was here.

He turned his head and said to Symmington, "I'll use this room if I may."

It was a small morning room with a window on the front of the house.

"Certainly, certainly."

Symmington's poise was pretty good, but he looked desperately tired. Superintendent Nash said gently:

"I should have some breakfast if I were you, Mr. Symmington. You and Miss Holland and Miss Megan will feel much better after coffee and eggs and bacon. Murder is a nasty business on an empty stomach."

He spoke in a comfortable family-doctor kind of way.

Symmington gave a faint attempt at a smile and said, "Thank you, Superintendent, I'll take your advice."

I followed Nash into the little morning room and he shut the door.

He said then, "You've got here very quickly? How did you hear?"

I told him that Megan had rung me up. I felt well-disposed toward Superintendent Nash. He, at any rate, had not forgotten that Megan, too, would be in need of breakfast.

"I hear that you telephoned last night, Mr. Burton, asking about this girl? Why was that?"

I suppose it did seem odd. I told him about Agnes' telephone call to Partridge and her nonappearance. He said, "Yes, I see. . . ."

He said it slowly and reflectively, rubbing his chin.

Then he sighed.

"Well," he said. "It's murder now, right enough. Direct physical action. The question is, what did the girl know? Did she say anything to this Partridge? Anything definite?"

"I don't think so. But you can ask her."

"Yes, I shall come up and see her when I've finished here."

"What happened exactly?" I asked. "Or don't you know yet?"

"Near enough. It was the maids' day out—"

"Both of them?"

"Yes, it seems that there used to be two sisters here who liked to go out together, so Mrs. Symmington arranged it that way. Then when these two came, she kept to the same arrangement. They used to have cold supper laid out in the dining room, and Miss Holland used to get tea."

"I see."

"It's pretty clear up to a point. The cook, Rose, comes from Nether Mickford, and in order to get there on her day out she has to catch the half-past-two bus. So Agnes has to finish clearing up lunch always. Rose used to wash up the supper things in the evenings to even things up.

"That's what happened today. Rose went off to catch the bus at two-twenty-five, Symmington left for his office at twenty-five to three. Elsie Holland and the children went out at a quarter to three. Megan Hunter went out on her bicycle about five minutes later. Agnes would then be alone in the house. As far as I can make out, she normally left the house between three o'clock and half past three."

"The house being then left empty?"

"Oh, they don't worry about that down here. There's not much locking up done in these parts. As I say, at ten minutes to three Agnes was alone in the house. That she never left it is clear, for she was in her cap and apron still when we found her body."

"I suppose you can tell roughly the time of death?"

"Doctor Griffith won't commit himself. Between two o'clock and four-thirty is his official medical verdict."

"How was she killed?"

"She was first stunned by a blow on the back of the head. Afterward an ordinary kitchen skewer, sharpened to a fine point, was thrust into the base of the skull, causing instantaneous death."

I lit a cigarette. It was not a nice picture.

"Pretty cold-blooded," I said.

"Oh, yes, yes, that was indicated."

I inhaled deeply.

"Who did it?" I said. "And why?"

"I don't suppose," said Nash slowly, "that we shall ever know exactly why. But we can guess."

"She knew something?"

"She knew something."

"She didn't give anyone here a hint?"

"As far as I can make out, no. She's been upset, so the cook says, ever since Mrs. Symmington's death, and according to this Rose, she's been getting more and more worried, and kept saying she didn't know what she ought to do."

He gave a short exasperated sigh.

"It's always the way. They won't come to us. They've got that deep-seated prejudice against 'being mixed up with the police.' If she'd come along and told us what was worrying her, she'd be alive today."

"Didn't she give the other women *any* hint?"

"No, or so Rose says, and I'm inclined to believe her. For if she had, Rose would have blurted it out at once with a good many fancy embellishments of her own."

"It's maddening," I said, "not to know."

"We can still guess, Mr. Burton. To begin with, it can't be anything very definite. It's got to be the sort of thing that you think over, and as you think it over, your uneasiness grows. You see what I mean?"

"Yes."

"Actually, I think I know what it was."

I looked at him with respect.

"That's good work, Superintendent."

"Well, you see, Mr. Burton, I know something that you don't. On the afternoon that Mrs. Symmington committed suicide both maids were supposed to be out. It was their day out. But actually Agnes came back to the house."

"You know that?"

"Yes. Agnes has a boy friend—young Rendell from the fish shop. Wednesday is early closing and he comes along to meet Agnes and they go for a walk, or to the pictures if it's wet. That Wednesday they had a row practically as soon as they met. Our letter writer had been active, suggesting that Agnes had other fish to fry, and young Fred Rendell was all worked up. They quarreled violently and Agnes bolted back home and said she wasn't coming out unless Fred said he was sorry.''

"Well?"

"Well, Mr. Burton, the kitchen faces the back of the house, but the pantry looks out where we are looking now. There's only one entrance gate. You come through it and either up to the front door, or else along the path at the side of the house to the back door.''

He paused.

"Now I'll tell you something: That letter that came to Mrs. Symmington that afternoon *didn't come by post.* It had a used stamp affixed to it, and the postmark faked quite convincingly in lamp black, so that it would seem to have been delivered by the postman with the afternoon letters. But actually *it had not been through the post.* You see what that means?''

"It means," I said slowly, "that it was left *by hand,* pushed through the letter box some time before the afternoon post was delivered, so that it should be among the other letters.''

"Exactly. The afternoon post comes around about a quarter to four. My theory is this: The girl was in the pantry looking through the window (it's masked by shrubs but you can see through them quite well) watching out for her young man to turn up and apologize.''

I said, *"And she saw whoever it was delivered that note?"*

"That's my guess, Mr. Burton. I may be wrong, of course."

"I don't think you are. . . . It's simple—and convincing—and it means that Agnes knew *who the anonymous letter writer was.*"

5

"Yes," Nash said. "Agnes knew who wrote those letters."

"But then why didn't she—?" I paused, frowning.

Nash said quickly, "As I see it, the girl *didn't realize what she had seen.* Not at first. Somebody had left a letter at the house, yes—but that somebody was nobody she would dream of connecting with the anonymous letters. It was somebody, from that point of view, quite above suspicion."

"But the more she thought about it, the more uneasy she grew. Ought she, perhaps, to tell someone about it? In her perplexity she thinks of Miss Barton's Partridge who, I gather, is a somewhat dominant personality and whose judgment Agnes would accept unhesitatingly. She decides to ask Partridge what she ought to do."

"Yes," I said thoughtfully. "It fits well enough. And somehow or other, Poison Pen found out. How did she find out, Superintendent?''

"You're not used to living in the country, Mr. Burton. It's a kind of miracle how things get around. First of all there's the telephone call. Who overheard it on your end?''

I reflected.

"I took the call originally. I called up to Partridge.''

"Mentioning the girl's name?''

"Yes—yes, I did.''

"Anyone overhear you?''

"My sister or Miss Griffith might have done so.''

"Ah, Miss Griffith. What was she doing up there?''

I explained.

"Was she going back to the village?''

"She was going to Mr. Pye first.''

Superintendent Nash sighed. "That's two ways it could have gone all over the place.''

I was incredulous. "Do you mean that either Miss Griffith or Mr. Pye would bother to repeat a meaningless little bit of information like that?''

"Anything's news in a place like this. You'd be surprised. If the dressmaker's mother has got a bad corn everybody hears about it! And then there is this end. Miss Holland, Rose—they could have heard what Agnes said. And there's Fred Rendell. It may have got around through him that Agnes went back to the house that afternoon.''

I gave a slight shiver. I was looking out of the window. In front of me was a neat square of grass and a path and the low prim gate.

Someone had opened the gate, had walked very correctly and quietly up to the house, and had pushed a letter through the letter box. I saw, hazily, in my mind's eye, that vague woman's shape. The face was blank—but it must be a face that I knew . . .

Superintendent Nash was saying:

"All the same, this narrows things down. That's always the way we get 'em in the end. Steady, patient elimination. There aren't so very many people it could be now."

"You mean—?"

"It knocks out any women clerks who were at their work all the afternoon. It knocks out the schoolmistress. She was teaching. And the district nurse. I know where she was yesterday. Not that I ever thought it was any of *them*, but now we're *sure*. You see, Mr. Burton, we've got two definite times now on which to concentrate—yesterday afternoon, and the week before. On the day of Mrs. Symmington's death from, say, a quarter past three (the earliest possible time at which Agnes could have been back in the house after her quarrel) and four o'clock when the post must have come (but I can get that fixed more accurately with the postman). And yesterday from ten minutes to three (when Miss Megan Hunter left the house) until half past three or more probably a quarter past three as Agnes hadn't begun to change."

"What do you think happened yesterday?"

Nash made a grimace.

"What do I think? I think a certain lady walked up to the front door and rang the bell, quite calm and smiling, the afternoon caller. . . . Maybe she asked for Miss Holland, or for Miss Megan, or perhaps she had brought a parcel. Anyway Agnes turns around to get a salver for cards, or to take the parcel in, and our ladylike caller bats her on the back of her unsuspecting head.''

"What with?''

Nash said, ''The ladies around here usually carry large sizes in handbags. No saying what mightn't be inside it.''

"And then stabs her through the back of the neck and bundles her into the cupboard? Wouldn't that be a hefty job for a woman?''

Superintendent Nash looked at me with rather a queer expression. ''The woman we're after isn't normal—not by a long way—and that type of mental instability goes with surprising strength. Agnes wasn't a big girl!'' He paused and then asked, ''What made Miss Megan Hunter think of looking in that cupboard?''

"Sheer instinct,'' I said.

Then I asked, ''Why drag her out of the way? What was the point?''

"The longer it was before the body was found, the more difficult it would be to fix the time of death accurately. If Miss Holland, for instance, fell over the body as soon as she came in, a doctor might be able to fix it within ten minutes or so— which might be awkward for our lady friend.''

I said, frowning, ''But if Agnes was suspicious of this person—''

Nash interrupted me: ''She wasn't. Not to this pitch. She just thought it 'queer' shall we say? She was a slow-witted girl, I imagine, and she was only vaguely suspicious with a feeling that something was wrong. She certainly didn't suspect that she was up against a woman who would do murder.''

"Did you suspect that?'' I asked.

Nash shook his head. He said, with feeling:

"I ought to have known. That suicide business,

you see, frightened Poison Pen. She got the wind up. Fear, Mr. Burton, is an incalculable thing."

Yes, fear. That was the thing we ought to have foreseen. Fear—in a lunatic brain. . . .

"You see," said Superintendent Nash, and somehow his words made the whole thing seem absolutely horrible. "We're up against someone who's respected and thought highly of—someone, in fact, of good social position!"

Presently Nash said that he was going to interview Rose once more. I asked him, rather diffidently, if I might come too. Rather to my surprise he assented cordially.

"I'm very glad of your co-operation, Mr. Burton, if I may say so."

"That sounds suspicious," I said. "In books when a detective welcomes someone's assistance, that someone is usually the murderer."

Nash laughed shortly. He said, "You're hardly the type to write anonymous letters, Mr. Burton." He added: "Frankly, you can be useful to us."

"I'm glad, but I don't see how."

"You're a stranger down her, that's why. You've got no preconceived ideas about the people here. But at the same time, you've got the opportunity of getting to know things in what I may call a social way."

"The murderer is a person of good social position," I murmured.

"Exactly."

"I'm to be the spy within the gates?"

"Have you any objection?"

I thought it over. "No," I said, "frankly I haven't. If there's a dangerous lunatic about, driving inoffensive women to suicide and hitting miserable little maidservants on the head, then I'm not averse to doing a bit of dirty work to put that lunatic under restraint.''

"That's sensible of you, sir. And let me tell you, the person we're after is dangerous. She's about as dangerous as a rattlesnake and a cobra and a black mamba rolled into one.''

I gave a slight shiver. I said, "In fact, we've got to make haste?''

"That's right. Don't think we're inactive in the force. We're not. We're working on several different lines.''

He said it grimly.

I had a vision of a fine, far-flung spider's web . . .

Nash wanted to hear Rose's story again, so he explained to me, because she had already told him two different versions, and the more versions he got from her, the more likely it was that a few grains of truth might be incorporated.

We found Rose washing up breakfast, and she stopped at once and rolled her eyes and clutched her heart and explained again how she'd been coming over queer all the morning.

Nash was patient with her but firm. He'd been soothing the first time, so he told me, and peremptory the second, and he now employed a mixture of the two.

Rose enlarged pleasurably on the details of the past week, of how Agnes had gone about in deadly fear, and had shivered and said "Don't ask me" when Rose had urged her to say what was the matter. "It would be death if she told me, that's what she said,'' finished Rose, rolling her eyes happily.

"Had Agnes given no hint of what was troubling her?''

No, except that she went in fear of her life.

Superintendent Nash sighed and abandoned the theme, contenting himself with extracting an exact account of Rose's own activities the preceding afternoon.

This, put baldly, was that Rose had caught the 2:30 bus and had spent the afternoon and evening with her family, returning by the 8:40 bus from Nether Mickford. The recital was complicated by the extraordinary presentiments of evil that Rose had had all the afternoon and how her sister had commented on it and how she hadn't been able to touch a morsel of seed cake.

From the kitchen we went in search of Elsie Holland, who was superintending the children's lessons.

As always, Elsie Holland was competent and obliging. She rose and said, "Now, Colin, you and Brian will do these three sums and have the answers ready for me when I come back."

She then led us into the night nursery.

"Will this do? I thought it would be better not to talk before the children."

"Thank you, Miss Holland. Just tell me, once more, are you *quite* sure that Agnes never mentioned to you being worried over anything—since Mrs. Symmington's death, I mean?"

"No, she never said anything. She was a very quiet girl, you know, and didn't talk much."

"A change from the other one, then!"

"Yes, Rose talks much too much. I have to tell her not to be impertinent sometimes."

"Now, will you tell me exactly what happened yesterday afternoon? Everything you can remember."

"Well, we had lunch as usual. One o'clock, and

we hurried just a little. I don't let the boys dawdle. Let me see. Mr. Symmington went back to the office, and I helped Agnes by laying the table for supper—the boys ran out in the garden till I was ready to take them.''

"Where did you go?"

"Toward Combe Acre, by the field path—the boys wanted to fish. I forgot their bait and had to go back for it."

"What time was that?"

"Let me see, we started about twenty to three— or just after. Megan was coming but changed her mind. She was going out on her bicycle. She's got quite a craze for bicycling."

"I mean what time was it when you went back for the bait? Did you go into the house?"

"No. I'd left it in the conservatory at the back. I don't know what time it was then—about ten minutes to three, perhaps."

"Did you see Megan or Agnes?"

"Megan must have started, I think. No, I didn't see Agnes. I didn't see anyone."

"And after that you went fishing?"

"Yes, we went along by the stream. We didn't catch anything. We hardly ever do, but the boys enjoy it. Brian got rather wet. I had to change his things when we got in."

"You attend to tea on Wednesdays?"

"Yes. It's all ready in the drawing room for Mr. Symmington. I just make the tea when he comes in. The children and I have ours in the schoolroom—and Megan, of course. I have my own tea things and everything in the cupboard up there."

"What time did you get in?"

"At ten minutes to five. I took the boys up and started to lay tea. Then when Mr. Symmington came in at five I went down to make his but he said he would have it with us in the schoolroom. The boys were so pleased. We played Animal Grab afterward. It seems so awful to think of now—with that poor girl in the cupboard all the time."

"Would anybody go to that cupboard normally?"

"Oh, no, it's only used for keeping junk. The hats and coats hang in the little cloakroom to the right of the front door as you come in. No one might have gone to the other cupboard for months."

"I see. And you noticed nothing unusual, nothing abnormal at all when you came back?"

The blue eyes opened very wide. "Oh, no, Inspector, nothing at all. Everything was just the same as usual. That's what was so awful about it."

"And the week before?"

"You mean the day Mrs. Symmington—"

"Yes."

"Oh, that was terrible—terrible!"

"Yes, yes, I know. You were out all that afternoon also?"

"Oh, yes, I always take the boys out in the afternoon—if it's fine enough. We do lessons in the morning. We went up on the moor, I remember—quite a long way. I was afraid I was late back because as I turned in at the gate I saw Mr. Symmington coming from his office at the other end of the road, and I hadn't even put the kettle on, but it was just ten minutes to five."

"You didn't go up to Mrs. Symmington?"

"Oh, no. I never did. She always rested after lunch. She had attacks of neuralgia—and they used to come on after meals. Dr. Griffith had given her some powders to take. She used to lie down and try to sleep.''

Nash said in a casual voice, ''So no one would take her up the post?''

''The afternoon post? No, I'd look in the letter box and put the letters on the hall table when I came in. But very often Mrs. Symmington used to come down and get it herself. She didn't sleep all the afternoon. She was usually up again by four.''

''You didn't think anything was wrong because she wasn't up that afternoon?''

''Oh, no, I never dreamed of such a thing. Mr. Symmington was hanging up his coat in the hall and I said, 'Tea's not quite ready, but the kettle's nearly boiling,' and he nodded and called out, 'Mona, Mona!'—and then as Mrs. Symmington didn't answer he went upstairs to her bedroom, and it must have been the most terrible shock to him. He called me and I came, and he said, 'Keep the children away,' and then he phoned Dr. Griffith and we forgot all about the kettle and it burned the bottom out! Oh, dear, it *was* dreadful, and she'd been so happy and cheerful at lunch.''

Nash said abruptly, ''What is your own opinion of that letter she received, Miss Holland?''

Elsie Holland said indignantly, ''Oh, I think it was wicked—wicked!''

''Yes, yes, I don't mean that. Did you think it was true?''

Elsie Holland said firmly:

''No, indeed I don't. Mrs. Symmington was very sensitive—very sensitive indeed. She had to take all sorts of things for her nerves. And she was very—well, *particular*.'' Elsie flushed. ''Anything of that sort—*nasty*, I mean—would have given her a great shock.''

Nash was silent for a moment, then he asked: ''Have you had any of these letters, Miss Holland?''

''No. No, I haven't had any.''

''Are you sure? Please''—he lifted a hand—''don't answer in a hurry. They're not pleasant things to get, I know. And sometimes people don't like to admit they've had them. But it's very important in this case that we should know. We're quite aware that the statements in them are just a tissue of lies, so you needn't feel embarrassed.''

''But I haven't, Superintendent. Really I haven't. Not anything of the kind.''

She was indignant, almost tearful, and her denials seemed genuine enough.

When she went back to the children, Nash stood looking out of the window.

''Well,'' he said, ''that's that! She says she hasn't received any of these letters. And she sounds as though she's speaking the truth.''

''She did certainly. I'm sure she was.''

''H'm,'' said Nash. ''Then what I want to know is, why the devil hasn't she?''

He went on rather impatiently, as I stared at him:

''She's a pretty girl, isn't she?''

''Rather more than pretty.''

''Exactly. As a matter of fact, she's uncommonly good-looking. And she's young. In fact she's just the meat an anonymous letter writer would like. Then why has she been left out?''

I shook my head.

''It's interesting, you know. I must mention it

to Graves. He asked if we could tell him definitely of anyone who hadn't had one."

"She's the second person," I said. "There's Emily Barton, remember."

Nash gave a faint chuckle. "You shouldn't believe everything you're told, Mr. Burton. Miss Barton had one all right—more than one."

"How do you know?"

"That devoted dragon she's lodging with told me—her late parlormaid or cook. Florence Elford. Very indignant she was about it. Would like to have the writer's blood."

"Why did Miss Emily say she hadn't had any?"

"Delicacy. Their language isn't nice. Little Miss Barton has spent her life avoiding the coarse and unrefined."

"What did the letter say?"

"The usual. Quite ludicrous in her case. And incidentally insinuated that she poisoned off her old mother and most of her sisters!"

I said incredulously, "Do you mean to say there's really this dangerous lunatic going about and we can't spot her right away?"

"We'll spot her," said Nash, and his voice was grim. "She'll write just one letter too many."

"But, my goodness, man, she won't go on writing these things—not now."

He looked at me.

"Oh, yes, she will. You see, *she can't stop now.* It's a morbid craving. The letters will go on, make no mistake about that."

I went and found Megan before leaving the house. She was in the garden and seemed almost back to her usual self. She greeted me quite cheerfully.

I suggested that she should come back to us again for a while, but after a momentary hesitation she shook her head.

"It's nice of you—but I think I'll stay here. After all, it is—well, I suppose it's my home. And I dare say I can help with the boys a bit."

"Well," I said, "it's as you like."

"Then I think I'll stay. I could—I could—"

"Yes?" I prompted.

"If—if anything awful happened, I could ring you up, couldn't I, and you'd come."

I was touched. "Of course. But what awful thing do you think might happen?"

"Oh, I don't know." She looked vague. "Things seem rather like that just now, don't they?"

"Stop it!" I said. "And don't go nosing out any more bodies! It's not good for you."

She gave me a brief flash of a smile. "No, it isn't. It made me feel awfully sick."

I didn't much like leaving her there, but after all, as she had said, it was her home. And I fancied now that Elsie Holland would feel more responsible for her.

Nash and I went up together to Little Furze. While I gave Joanna an account of the morning's doings, Nash tackled Partridge. He rejoined us, looking discouraged.

"Not much help there. According to this woman, the girl only said she was worried about something and didn't know what to do and that she'd like Miss Partridge's advice."

"Did Partridge mention the fact to anyone?" asked Joanna.

Nash nodded, looking grim.

"Yes, she told Mrs. Emory—your daily woman

—on the lines, as far as I can gather, that there were *some* young women who were willing to take advice from their elders and didn't think they could settle everything for themselves offhand! Agnes mightn't be very bright, but she was a nice respectful girl and knew her manners."

"Partridge preening herself, in fact," murmured Joanna. "And Mrs. Emory could have passed it around the town?"

"That's right, Miss Burton."

"There's one thing rather surprises me," I said. "Why were my sister and I included? We were strangers down here—nobody could have had a grudge against us."

"You're failing to allow for the mentality of a Poison Pen—all is grist that comes to their mill. Their grudge, you might say, is against humanity."

"I suppose," said Joanna thoughtfully, "that that is what Mrs. Dane Calthrop meant."

Nash looked at her inquiringly, but she did not enlighten him.

The superintendent said:

"I don't know if you happened to look closely at the envelope of the letter you got, Miss Burton. If so, you may have noticed that it was actually addressed to Miss Barton, and the *a* altered to a *u* afterward.

That remark, properly interpreted, ought to have given us a clue to the whole business. As it was, none of us saw any significance in it.

Nash went off, and I was left with Joanna. She actually said: "You don't think that letter can really have been meant for Miss Emily, do you?"

"It would hardly have begun 'You painted

trollop,' " I pointed, and Joanna agreed.

Then she suggested that I should go down to the town. "You ought to hear what everyone is saying. It will be *the* topic this morning!"

I suggested that she should come too, but rather to my surprise Joanna refused. She said she was going to mess about in the garden.

I paused in the doorway and said, lowering my voice, "I suppose Partridge is all right."

"Partridge!"

The amazement in Joanna's voice made me feel ashamed of my idea.

I said apologetically, "I just wondered. She's rather 'queer' in some ways—a grim spinster—the sort of person who might have religious mania."

"This isn't religious mania—or so you told me Graves said."

"Well, sex mania. They're very closely tied up together, I understand. She's repressed and respectable, and has been shut up here with a lot of elderly women for years."

"What put the idea into your head?"

"Well," I said slowly, "we've only her word for it, haven't we, as to what the girl Agnes said to her? Suppose Agnes asked Partridge to tell her why Partridge came and left a note that day—and Partridge said she'd call around that afternoon and explain."

"And then camouflaged it by coming to us and asking if the girl could come here?"

"Yes."

"But she never went out that afternoon."

"You don't know that. We were out ourselves, remember."

"Yes, that's true. It's possible, I suppose."

Joanna turned it over in her mind. "But I don't think so, all the same. I don't think Partridge has the mentality to cover her tracks over the letters. To wipe off fingerprints, and all that. It isn't only cunning you want—it's knowledge. I don't think she's got that. I suppose—" Joanna hesitated, then said slowly, "they are sure it is a woman, aren't they?"

"You don't think it's a man?" I exclaimed incredulously.

"Not—not an ordinary man—but a certain kind of man. I'm thinking, really, of Mr. Pye."

"So Pye is your selection?"

"Don't you feel yourself that he's a possibility? He's the sort of person who might be lonely—and unhappy—and spiteful. Everyone, you see, rather laughs at him. Can't you see him secretly hating all the normal happy people, and taking a queer, perverse, artistic pleasure in what he was doing?"

"Graves said a middle-aged spinster."

"Mr. Pye," said Joanna, "*is* a middle-aged spinster."

"A misfit," I said slowly.

"Very much so. He's rich, but money doesn't help. And I do feel he might be unbalanced. He is, really, rather a *frightening* little man."

"He got a letter himself, remember."

"We don't know that," Joanna pointed out. "We only thought so. And anyway, he might have been putting on an act."

"For our benefit?"

"Yes. He's clever enough to think of that—and not to overdo it."

"He must be a first-class actor."

"But of course, Jerry, whoever is doing this

must be a first-class actor. That's partly where the pleasure comes in.''

"For heaven's sake, Joanna, don't speak so understandingly! You make me feel that you— that you understand the mentality.''

"I think I do. I can—just—get into the mood. If I wasn't Joanna Burton, if I wasn't young and reasonably attractive and able to have a good time, if I was—how shall I put it?—behind bars, watching other people enjoy life, would a black, evil tide rise in me, making me want to hurt, to torture—even to destroy?''

"Joanna!" I took her by the shoulders and shook her. She gave a little sigh and shiver, and smiled at me.

"I frightened you, didn't I, Jerry? But I have a feeling that that's the right way to solve this problem. You've got to be the person, knowing how they feel and what makes them act, and then—and then perhaps you'll know what they're going to do next.''

"Oh, gee!" I said. "And I came down here to be a vegetable and get interested in all the dear little local scandals. Dear little local scandals! Libel, vilification, obscene language and murder!''

Joanna was quite right. The High Street was full of interesting groups. I was determined to get everyone's reactions in turn.

I met Griffith first. He looked terribly ill and tired. So much so that I wondered. Murder is not, certainly, all in the day's work to a doctor, but his profession does equip him to face most things including suffering, the ugly side of human nature, and the fact of death.

"You look all in," I said.

"Do I?" He was vague. "Oh! I've had some worrying cases lately."

"Including our lunatic at large?"

"That, certainly." He looked away from me across the street. I saw a fine nerve twitching in his eyelid.

"You've no suspicions as to—*who*?"

"No. No. I wish I had."

He asked abruptly after Joanna and said, hesitatingly, that he had some photographs she'd wanted to see.

I offered to take them to her.

"Oh, it doesn't matter. I shall be passing that way actually later in the morning."

I began to be afraid that Griffith had got it badly. Curse Joanna! Griffith was too good a man to be dangled as a scalp.

I let him go, for I saw his sister coming and I wanted, for once, to talk to her.

Aimée Griffith began, as it were, in the middle of conversation. "Absolutely shocking!" she boomed. "I hear you were there—quite early?"

There was a question in the words, and her eyes glinted as she stressed the word "early." I wasn't going to tell her that Megan had rung me up. I said instead, "You see, I was a bit uneasy last night. The girl was due to tea at our house and didn't turn up."

"And so you feared the worst? Very smart of you!"

"Yes," I said. "I'm quite the human bloodhound."

"It's the first murder we've ever had in Lymstock. Excitement is terrific. Hope the police can handle it all right."

"I shouldn't worry," I said. "They're an efficient body of men."

"Can't even remember what the girl looked like, although I suppose she's opened the door to me dozens of times. Quiet, insignificant little thing. Knocked on the head and then stabbed through the back of the neck, so Owen tells me. Looks like a boy friend to me. What do you think?"

"That's your solution?"

"Seems the most likely one. Had a quarrel, I expect. They're very inbred around here—bad heredity, a lot of them." She paused, and then went on: "I hear Megan Hunter found the body? Must have given her a bit of a shock."

I said shortly, "It did."

"Not too good for her, I should imagine. In my opinion she's not too strong in the head—and a thing like this might send her completely off her onion."

I took a sudden resolution. I had to know something.

"Tell me, Miss Griffith, was it you who persuaded Megan to return home yesterday?"

"Well, I wouldn't say exactly persuaded."

I stuck to my guns. "But you did say something to her?"

Aimée Griffith planted her feet firmly and stared me in the eyes. She was, just slightly, on the defensive. She said:

"It's no good—that young woman shirking her responsibility. She's young and she doesn't know how tongues wag, so I felt it my duty to give her a hint."

"Tongues—?" I broke off because I was too angry to go on.

Aimée Griffith continued with that maddeningly complacent confidence in herself which was her chief characteristic:

"Oh, I dare say you don't hear all the gossip that goes around. I do! I know what people are saying. Mind you, I don't for a minute think there's anything in it—not for a minute! But you know what people are—if they can say something ill-natured, they do! And it's rather hard lines on the girl when she's got her living to earn."

"Her living to earn?" I said, puzzled.

Aimée went on:

"It's a difficult position for her, naturally. And I think she did the right thing. I mean, she couldn't go off at a moment's notice and leave the children with no one to look after them. She's been splendid—absolutely splendid. I say so to everybody! But there it is, it's an invidious position, and people will talk."

"Who are you talking about?" I asked.

"Elsie Holland, of course," said Aimée Griffith impatiently. "In my opinion, she's a thoroughly nice girl and has only been doing her duty."

"And what are people saying?"

Aimée Griffith laughed. It was, I thought, rather an unpleasant laugh.

"They're saying that she's already considering the possibility of becoming Mrs. Symmington No. 2—that she's all out to console the widower and make herself indispensable."

"But," I said, shocked, "Mrs. Symmington's only been dead a week!"

Aimée Griffith shrugged her shoulders.

"Of course. It's absurd! But you know what people are! The Holland girl is young and she's good-looking—that's enough. And mind you, being a nursery governess isn't much of a prospect for a girl. I wouldn't blame her if she wanted a settled home and a husband who was playing her cards accordingly.

"Of course," she went on. "Poor Dick Symmington hasn't the least idea of all this! He's still completely knocked out by Mona Symmington's death. But you know what men are! If the girl is always there, making him comfortable, looking after him, being obviously devoted to the children —well, he gets to be dependent on her."

I said quietly, "So you do think that Elsie Holland is a designing hussy?"

Aimée Griffith flushed.

"Not at all. I'm sorry for the girl—with people saying nasty things! That's why I more or less told Megan that she ought to go home. It looks better than having Dick Symmington and the girl alone in the house."

I began to understand things.

Aimée Griffith gave her jolly laugh. "You're shocked, Mr. Burton, at hearing what our gossiping little town thinks. I can tell you this—they always think the worst!"

She laughed and nodded and strode away.

I came upon Mr. Pye by the church. He was talking to Emily Barton, who looked pink and excited.

Mr. Pye greeted me with every evidence of delight:

"Ah, Burton, good morning, good morning! How is your charming sister?"

I told him that Joanna was well.

"But not joining our village Parliament? We are all agog over the news. Murder! Real Sunday newspaper murder in our midst! Not the most interesting of crimes, I fear. Somewhat sordid. The brutal murder of a little serving maid. No finer points about the crime, but still undeniably news."

Miss Barton said tremulously, "It is shocking—quite shocking."

Mr. Pye turned on her: "But you enjoy it, dear lady, you enjoy it. Confess it now. You disapprove, you deplore, but there *is* the thrill. I insist, there *is* the thrill!"

"Such a nice girl," said Emily Barton. "She came to me from St. Clotilde's Home. Quite a raw girl. But most teachable. She turned into such a nice little maid. Partridge was very pleased with her."

I said quickly, "She was coming to tea with Partridge yesterday afternoon." I turned to Pye: "I expect Aimée Griffith told you."

My tone was quite casual. Pye responded apparently quite unsuspiciously:

"She did mention it, yes. She said, I remember, that it was something quite new for servants to ring up on their employers' telephones."

"Partridge would never dream of doing such a thing," said Miss Emily, "and I am really surprised at Agnes doing so."

"You are behind the times, dear lady," said Mr. Pye. "My two terrors use the telephone constantly and smoked all over the house until I objected. But one daren't say too much. Prescott is a divine cook, though temperamental, and Mrs. Prescott is an admirable house-parlor maid."

"Yes, indeed, we all think you're very lucky."

I intervened, since I did not want the conversation to become purely domestic.

"The news of the murder has got around very quickly," I said.

"Of course, of course," said Mr. Pye. "The butcher, the baker, the candlestick maker. Enter Rumor, painted full of tongues! Lymstock, alas! is going to the dogs. Anonymous letters, murders, any amount of criminal tendencies."

Emily Barton said nervously, "They don't think—there's no idea—that—that the two are connected."

Mr. Pye pounced on the idea. "An interesting speculation. The girl knew something, therefore she was murdered. Yes, yes, most promising. How clever of you to think of it."

"I—I can't bear it."

Emily Barton spoke abruptly and turned away, walking very fast.

Pye looked after her. Her cherubic face was pursed up quizzically.

He turned back to me and shook his head gently.

"A sensitive soul. A charming creature, don't you think? Absolutely a period piece. She's not, you know, of her own generation, she's of the generation before that. The mother must have been a woman of very strong character. She kept the family time ticking at about 1870, I should say. The whole family preserved under a glass case. I do like to come across that sort of thing."

I did not want to talk about period pieces.

"What do you really think about all this business?" I asked.

"Meaning by that?"

"Anonymous letters, murder . . ."

"Our local crime wave? What do you?"

"I asked you first," I said pleasantly.

Mr. Pye said gently:

"I'm a student, you know, of abnormalities. They interest me. Such apparently unlikely people do the most fantastic things. Take the case of Lizzie Borden. There's not really a reasonable explanation of that. In this case, my advice to the police would be—study *character*. Leave your fingerprints and your measuring of handwriting and your microscopes. Notice instead what people do with their hands, and their little tricks of manner, and the way they eat their food, and if they laugh sometimes for no apparent reason."

I raised my eyebrows.

"Mad?" I said.

"Quite, quite mad," said Mr. Pye, and added, "but you'd never know it!"

"Who?"

His eyes met mine. He smiled.

"No, no, Burton, that would be slander. We can't add slander to all the rest of it."

He fairly skipped off down the street.

6

As I stood staring after Mr. Pye the church door opened and the Rev. Caleb Dane Calthrop came out.

He smiled vaguely at me. "Good—good morning, Mr.—er—er—"

I helped him.

"Burton."

"Of course, of course, you mustn't think I don't remember you. Your name had just slipped my memory for the moment. A beautiful day."

"Yes," I said rather shortly.

He peered at me.

"But something—something, ah, yes, that poor unfortunate child who was in service at the Symmington's. I find it hard to believe, I must confess, that we have a murderer in our midst, Mr.—er—Burton."

"It does seem a bit fantastic," I said.

"Something else has just reached my ears." He leaned toward me. "I learn that there have been

anonymous letters going about. Have you heard
any rumor of such things?''

"I have heard," I said.

"Cowardly and dastardly things." He paused
and quoted an enormous stream of Latin. "Those
words of Horace are very applicable, don't you
think?" he said.

"Absolutely," I said.

There didn't seem anyone more I could profit-
ably talk to, so I went home, dropping in for some
tobacco and for a bottle of sherry, so as to get
some of the humbler opinions on the crime.

"A narsty tramp," seemed to be the verdict.

"Come to the door, they do, and whine and ask
for money, and then if it's a girl alone in the
house, they turn nasty. My sister Dora, over to
Combe Acre, she had a narsty experience one day
—drunk, he was, and selling those little printed
poems. . . ."

The story went on, ending with the intrepid
Dora courageously banging the door in the man's
face and taking refuge and barricading herself in
some vague retreat, which I gathered from the
delicacy in mentioning it, must be the lavatory.
"And there she stayed till her lady came home!"

I reached Little Furze just a few minutes before
lunch time. Joanna was standing in the drawing-
room window doing nothing at all and looking as
though her thoughts were miles away.

"What have you been doing with yourself?" I
asked.

"Oh, I don't know. Nothing particular."

I went out on the veranda. Two chairs were
drawn up to an iron table and there were two
empty sherry glasses. On another chair was an

object at which I looked with bewilderment for some time.

"What on earth is this?"

"Oh," said Joanna, "I think it's a photograph of a diseased spleen or something. Dr. Griffith seemed to think I'd be interested to see it."

I looked at the photograph with some interest. Every man has his own ways of courting the female sex. I should not, myself, choose to do it with photographs of spleens, diseased or otherwise. Still no doubt Joanna had asked for it!

"It looks most unpleasant," I said.

Joanna said it did, rather.

"How was Griffith?" I asked.

"He looked tired and very unhappy. I think he's got something on his mind."

"A spleen that won't yield to treatment?"

"Don't be silly. I mean something real."

"I should say the man's got *you* on his mind. I wish you'd lay off him, Joanna."

"Oh, do shut up. I haven't done anything."

"Women always say that."

Joanna whirled angrily out of the room.

The diseased spleen was beginning to curl up in the sun. I took it by one corner and brought it in to the drawing room. I had no affection for it myself, but I presumed it was one of Griffith's treasures.

I stooped down and pulled out a heavy book from the bottom shelf of the bookcase in order to press the photograph flat between its leaves. It was a ponderous volume of somebody's sermons.

The book came open in my hand in rather a surprising way. In another minute I saw why. *From the middle of it a number of pages had been neatly cut out.*

• • •

I stood staring at it. I looked at the title page. It had been published in 1840.

There could be no doubt at all. I was looking at the book from the pages of which the anonymous letters had been put together. Who had cut them out?

Well, to begin with, it could be Emily Barton herself. She was, perhaps, the obvious person to think of. Or it could have been Partridge.

But there were other possibilities. The pages could have been cut out by anyone who had been alone in this room, any visitor, for instance, who had sat there waiting for Miss Emily. Or even anyone who called on business.

No, that wasn't so likely. I had noticed that when, one day, a clerk from the bank had come to see me, Partridge had shown him into the little study at the back of the house. That was clearly the house routine.

A visitor, then? Someone "of good social position." Mr. Pye? Aimée Griffith? Mrs. Dane Calthrop?

The gong sounded and I went in to lunch. Afterward, in the drawing room I showed Joanna my find.

We discussed it from every aspect. Then I took it down to the police station.

They were elated at the find, and I was patted on the back for what was, after all, the sheerest piece of luck.

Graves was not there, but Nash was, and rang up the other man. They would test the book for fingerprints, though Nash was not hopeful of finding anything. I may say that he did not. There were mine, Partridge's and nobody else's, merely showing that Partridge dusted conscientiously.

Nash walked back with me up the hill. I asked how he was getting on.

"We're narrowing it down, Mr. Burton. We've eliminated the people it couldn't be."

"Ah," I said. "And who remains?"

"Miss Ginch. She was to meet a client at a house yesterday afternoon by appointment. That house was situated not far along the Combe Acre road—that's the road that goes past the Symmingtons'. She would have to pass the house both going and coming . . . the week before, the day the anonymous letter was delivered and Mrs. Symmington committed suicide, was her last day at Symmington's office.

"Mr. Symmington thought at first she had not left the office at all that afternoon. He had Sir Henry Lushington with him all the afternoon and rang several times for Miss Ginch. I find, however, that she did leave the office between three and four. She went out to get some high denomination of stamp of which they had run short. The office boy could have gone, but Miss Ginch elected to go, saying she had a headache and would like the air. She was not gone long."

"But long enough?"

"Yes, long enough to hurry along to the other end of the village, slip the letter in the box and hurry back. I must say, however, that I cannot find anybody who saw her near the Symmingtons' house."

"Would they notice?"

"They might and they might not."

"Who else is in your bag?"

Nash looked very straight ahead of him. "You'll

understand that we can't exclude anybody—anybody at all.''

"No," I said. "I see that."

He said gravely, "Miss Griffith went to Brenton for a meeting of Girl Guides yesterday. She arrived rather late."

"You don't think—"

"No, I don't think. But I don't *know*. Miss Griffith seems an eminently sane, healthy-minded woman—but I say, I don't *know*."

"What about the previous week? Could she have slipped the letter in the box?"

"It's possible. She was shopping in the town that afternoon." He paused. "The same applies to Miss Emily Barton. She was out shopping early yesterday afternoon and she went for a walk to see some friends on the road past the Symmingtons' house the week before."

I shook my head unbelievingly. Finding the cut book in Little Furze was bound, I knew, to direct attention to the owner of that house, but when I remembered Miss Emily coming in yesterday so bright and happy and excited . . .

Damn it all—excited. . . . Yes, excited—pink cheeks—shining eyes—surely not because—not because—

I said thickly, "This business is bad for one! One sees things—one imagines things—"

Nash nodded sympathetically. "Yes, it isn't very pleasant to look upon the fellow creatures one meets as possible criminal lunatics."

He paused for a moment, then went on, "And there's Mr. Pye—"

I said sharply, "So you have considered him?"

Nash smiled. "Oh, yes, we've considered him all right. A very curious character—not, I should say, a very nice character. He has no alibi. He was in his garden, alone, on both occasions.''

"So you're not only suspecting women?"

"I don't think a man wrote the letters—in fact, I'm sure of it—and so is Graves—always excepting our Mr. Pye, that is to say, who's got an abnormally female streak in his character. But we've checked up on *everybody* for yesterday afternoon. That's a murder case, you see. *You're* all right," he grinned, "and so's your sister, and Mr. Symmington didn't leave his office after he got there and Dr. Griffith was on a round in the other direction, and I've checked up on his visits."

He paused, smiled again, and said, "You see, we *are* thorough."

I said slowly: "So your case is eliminated down to those three? Mr. Pye, Miss Griffith, little Miss Barton?"

"Oh, no, no, we've got a couple more—besides the vicar's lady."

"You've thought of *her*?"

"We've thought of *everybody*, but Mrs. Dane Calthrop is a little too openly mad, if you know what I mean. Still she *could* have done it. She was in a wood watching birds yesterday afternoon— and the birds can't speak for her."

He turned sharply as Owen Griffith came into the police station.

"Hullo, Nash. I heard you were around asking for me this morning. Anything important?"

"Inquest on Friday, if that suits you, Dr. Griffith."

"Right. Moresby and I are doing the P. M. tonight."

Nash said, "There's just one other thing, Dr. Griffith. Mrs. Symmington was taking some powders or something, that you prescribed for her—"

He paused.

Owen Griffith said interrogatively, "Yes?"

"Would an overdose of those powders have been fatal?"

"Certainly not," Griffith said drily. "Not unless she'd taken about twenty-five of them!"

"But you once warned her about exceeding the dose, so Miss Holland tells me."

"Oh, that, yes. Mrs. Symmington was the sort of woman who would go and overdo anything she was given—fancy that to take twice as much would do her twice as much good, and you don't want anyone to overdo even phenacetin or aspirin —bad for the heart. And anyway there's absolutely no doubt about the cause of death. It was cyanide."

"Oh, I know that—you don't get my meaning. I only thought that when committing suicide you'd prefer to take an overdose of a soporific rather than to feed yourself prussic acid."

"Oh, quite. On the other hand, prussic acid is more dramatic and is pretty certain to do the trick. With barbiturates, for instance, you can bring the victim around if only a short time has elapsed."

"I see; thank you, Dr. Griffith."

Griffith departed, and I said goodby to Nash. I went slowly up the hill home. Joanna was out—at least there was no sign of her, and there was an enigmatical memorandum scribbled on the telephone block presumably for the guidance of either Partridge or myself:

"If Dr. Griffith rings up, I can't go on Tuesday, but could manage Wednesday or Thursday."

I raised my eyebrows and went into the drawing

room. I sat down in the most comfortable arm-chair—(none of them were very comfortable, they tended to have straight backs and were reminiscent of the late Mrs. Barton)—stretched out my legs and tried to think the whole thing out.

With sudden annoyance I remembered that Owen's arrival had interrupted my conversation with the inspector, and that he had mentioned two other people as being possibilities.

I wondered who they were.

Partridge, perhaps, for one? After all, the cut book had been found in this house. And Agnes could have been struck down quite unsuspectingly by her guide and mentor. No, you couldn't eliminate Partridge.

But who was the other?

Somebody, perhaps, that I didn't know? Mrs. Cleat? The original local suspect?

I closed my eyes. I considered the four people, these strangely unlikely people, in turn: Gentle, frail little Emily Barton? What points were there actually against her? A starved life? Dominated and repressed from early childhood? Too many sacrifices asked of her? Her curious horror of discussing anything "not quite nice"? Was that actually a sign of inner preoccupation with just these themes? Was I getting too horribly Freudian? I remembered a doctor once telling me that the mutterings of gentle maiden ladies when going off under an anesthetic were a revelation. "You wouldn't think they knew such words!"

Aimée Griffith?

Surely nothing repressed or "inhibited" about her. Cheery, mannish, successful. A full, busy life. Yet Mrs. Dane Calthrop had said, "Poor thing!"

And there was something—something—some remembrance . . . Ah! I'd got it. Owen Griffith saying something like, "We had an outbreak of anonymous letters up north where I had a practice."

Had that been Aimée Griffith's work, too? Surely rather a coincidence. Two outbreaks of the same thing.

Stop a minute, they'd tracked down the author of those. Griffith had said so. A schoolgirl.

Cold it was suddenly—must be a draft, from the window. I turned uncomfortably in my chair. Why did I suddenly feel so queer and upset?

Go on thinking . . . Aimée Griffith? Perhaps it was Aimée Griffith, *not* that other girl? And Aimée had come down here and started her tricks again. And that was why Owen Griffith was looking so unhappy and hag-ridden. He suspected. Yes, he suspected. . . .

Mr. Pye? Not, somehow, a very nice little man. I could imagine him staging the whole business, laughing . . .

That telephone message on the telephone pad in the hall—why did I keep thinking of it? Griffith and Joanna—he was falling for her. No, that wasn't why the message worried me. It was something else. . . .

My senses were swimming, sleep was very near. I repeated idiotically to myself: "No smoke without fire. No smoke without fire. . . . That's it . . . it all links up together. . . ."

And then I was walking down the street with Megan, and Elsie Holland passed. She was dressed as a bride, and people were murmuring, "She's going to marry Dr. Griffith at last. Of course, they've been engaged secretly for years . . ."

There we were, in the church, and Dane Calthrop was reading the service in Latin.

And in the middle of it Mrs. Dane Calthrop jumped up and cried energetically, "It's got to be stopped, I tell you. It's got to be stopped!"

For a minute or two I didn't know whether I was asleep or awake. Then my brain cleared, and I realized I was in the drawing room of Little Furze and that Mrs. Dane Calthrop had just come through the window and was standing in front of me saying with nervous violence:

"It has got to be *stopped*, I tell you."

I jumped up. "I beg your pardon," I said. "I'm afraid I was asleep. What did you say?"

Mrs. Dane Calthrop beat one fist fiercely on the palm of her other hand. "It's got to be stopped. These letters! Murder! You can't go on having poor innocent children like Agnes Woddell *killed*!"

"You're quite right," I said. "But how do you propose to set about it?"

Mrs. Dane Calthrop said, "We've got to do something!"

I smiled, perhaps in rather a superior fashion. "And what do you suggest that we should do?"

"Get the whole thing cleared up! I said this wasn't a wicked place. I was wrong. It is."

I felt annoyed. "Yes, my dear woman," I said, not too politely, "but what are you going to *do*?"

Mrs. Dane Calthrop said, "Put a stop to it all, of course."

"The police are doing their best."

"If Agnes could be killed yesterday, their best isn't good enough."

"So you know better than they do?"

"Not at all. *I* don't know anything at all. That's

why I'm going to call in an expert."

I shook my head. "You can't do that. Scotland Yard will only take over on a demand from the chief constable of the county. Actually they *have* sent Graves."

"I don't mean *that* kind of an expert. I don't mean someone who knows about anonymous letters or even about murder. I mean someone who knows *people*. Don't you see? We want someone who knows a great deal about *wickedness*!"

It was a queer point of view. But it was, somehow, stimulating.

Before I could say anything more, Mrs. Dane Calthrop nodded her head at me and said in a quick, confident tone:

"I'm going to see about it right away."

And she went out of the window again.

The next week, I think, was one of the queerest times I have ever passed through. It had an odd dream quality. Nothing seemed real.

The inquest on Agnes Woddell was held and the curious of Lymstock attended *en masse*. No new facts came to light and the only possible verdict was returned: "Murder by person or persons unknown."

So poor little Agnes Woddell, having had her hour of limelight, was duly buried in the quiet old churchyard and life in Lymstock went on as before.

No, that last statement is untrue. Not as before. . . .

There was a half-scared, half-avid gleam in almost everybody's eye. Neighbor looked at neighbor. One thing had been brought out clearly at the inquest—it was most unlikely that any stranger had killed Agnes Woddell. No tramps or unknown men had been noticed or reported in the district. Somewhere, then, in Lymstock, walking down the High Street, shopping, passing the time of day, was a person who had cracked a defenseless girl's skull and driven a sharp skewer home to her brain.

And no one knew who that person was.

As I say, the days went on in a kind of dream. I looked at everyone I met in a new light, the light of a possible murderer. It was not an agreeable sensation!

And in the evenings, with the curtain drawn, Joanna and I sat talking, talking, arguing, going over in turn all the various possibilities that still seemed so fantastic and incredible.

Joanna held firm to her theory of Mr. Pye. I, after wavering a little, had gone back to my original suspect, Miss Ginch. But we went over the possible names again and again:

Mr. Pye?

Miss Ginch?

Mrs. Dane Calthrop?

Aimée Griffith?

Emily Barton?

Partridge?

And all the time, nervously, apprehensively, we waited for something to happen.

But nothing did happen. Nobody, so far as we knew, received any more letters. Nash made periodic appearances in the town but what he was doing and what traps the police were setting, I had no idea. Graves had gone again.

Emily Barton came to tea. Megan came to lunch. Owen Griffith went about his practice. We went and drank sherry with Mr. Pye. And we went to tea at the vicarage.

I was glad to find that Mrs. Dane Calthrop displayed none of the militant ferocity she had shown on the occasion of our last meeting. I think she had forgotten all about it.

She seemed now principally concerned with the destruction of white butterflies so as to preserve cauliflower and cabbage plants.

Our afternoon at the vicarage was really one of the most peaceful we had spent. It was an attractive old house and had a big, shabby, comfortable drawing room with faded rose cretonne. The Dane Calthrops had a guest staying with them, an amiable, elderly lady who was knitting something with white, fleecy wool. We had very good hot scones for tea, the vicar came in, and beamed placidly on us while he pursued his gentle erudite conversation. It was very pleasant.

I don't mean that we got away from the topic of the murder, because we didn't.

Miss Marple, the guest, was naturally thrilled by the subject. As she said apologetically:

"We have so little to talk about in the country!" She had made up her mind that the dead girl must have been just like her Edith.

"Such a nice little maid, and so willing, but sometimes just a *little* slow to take in things."

Miss Marple also had a cousin whose niece's sister-in-law had had a great deal of annoyance and trouble over some anonymous letters, so that, too, was very interesting to the charming old lady.

"But tell me, dear," she said to Mrs. Dane Calthrop, "what do the village people—I mean the townspeople—say? What do *they* think?"

"Mrs. Cleat still, I suppose," said Joanna.

"Oh, no," said Mrs. Dane Calthrop. "Not *now*."

Miss Marple asked who Mrs. Cleat was.

Joanna said she was the village witch.

"That's right, isn't it, Mrs. Dane Calthrop?"

The vicar murmured a long Latin quotation about, I think, the evil power of witches, to which we all listened in respectful and uncomprehending silence.

"She's a very silly woman," said his wife. "Likes to show off. Goes out to gather herbs and things at the full of the moon and takes care that everybody in the place knows about it."

"And silly girls go and consult her, I suppose?" said Miss Marple.

I saw the vicar getting ready to unload more Latin on us and I asked hastily, "But why shouldn't people suspect her of the murder now? They thought the letters were her doing."

Miss Marple said finally:

"Oh! But the girl was killed with a *skewer*, so I hear. Very unpleasant! Well, naturally, that takes *all* suspicion away from this Mrs. Cleat. Because, you see, she could ill-wish her, so that the girl would waste away and die from natural causes."

"Strange how those old beliefs linger," said the vicar. "In early Christian times, local superstitions were wisely incorporated with Christian doctrines and their most unpleasant attributes gradually eliminated."

"It isn't superstition we've got to deal with here," said Mrs. Dane Calthrop, "but *facts*."

"And very unpleasant facts," I said.

"As you say, Mr. Burton," said Miss Marple. "Now *you*—excuse me if I am being too personal—are a stranger here, and have a knowledge of the world and of various aspects of life. It seems to me that you ought to be able to find a solution to this distasteful problem.''

I smiled.

''The best solution I have had was a dream. In my dream it all fitted in and panned out beautifully. Unfortunately when I woke up the whole thing was nonsense!''

''How interesting, though. Do tell me how the nonsense went.''

''Oh, it all started with the silly phrase 'No smoke without fire.' People have been saying that *ad nauseam*. And then I got it mixed up with war terms. Smoke screen, scrap of paper, telephone messages—no, that was another dream.''

''And what was that dream?''

The old lady was so eager about it, that I felt sure she was a secret reader of Napoleon's Book of Dreams, which had been the great stand-by of my old nurse.

''Oh! Only Elsie Holland—the Symmingtons' nursery governess, you know, was getting married to Dr. Griffith and the vicar here was reading the service in Latin—('Very appropriate, dear,' murmured Mrs. Dane Calthrop to her spouse) and then Mrs. Dane Calthrop got up and forbade the banns and said it had got to be stopped!

''But that part,'' I added with a smile, ''was true. I woke up and found you standing over me saying it.''

''And I was quite right,'' said Mrs. Dane Calthrop—but quite mildly, I was glad to note.

''But where did a telephone message come in?'' asked Miss Marple, crinkling her brows.

''I'm afraid I'm being rather stupid. That wasn't in the dream. I was just before it. I came through the hall and noticed Joanna had written down a message to be given to someone if they rang up."

Miss Marple leaned forward. There was a pink spot in each cheek. "Will you think me *very* inquisitive and *very* rude if I ask just what that message was?" She cast a glance at Joanna. "I *do* apologize, my dear."

Joanna, however, was highly entertained.

"Oh, I don't mind," she assured the old lady. "I can't remember anything about it myself, but perhaps Jerry can. It must have been something quite trivial."

Solemnly I repeated the message as best I could remember it, enormously tickled at the old lady's rapt attention.

I was afraid the actual words were going to disappoint her, but perhaps she had some sentimental idea of a romance, for she nodded her head and smiled and seemed pleased.

"I see," she said. "I thought it might be something like that."

Mrs. Dane Calthrop said sharply, "Like what, Jane?"

"Something quite ordinary," said Miss Marple.

She looked at me thoughtfully for a moment or two, then she said unexpectedly, "I can see you are a very clever young man—but with not quite enough confidence in yourself. You ought to have!"

Joanna gave a loud hoot. "For goodness' sake don't encourage him to feel like that. He thinks quite enough of himself as it is."

"Be quiet, Joanna," I said. "Miss Marple understands me."

Miss Marple had resumed her fleecy knitting.

"You know," she observed pensively, "to commit a successful murder must be very much like bringing off a conjuring trick."

"The quickness of the hand deceives the eye?"

"Not only that. You've got to make people look at the wrong thing and in the wrong place—misdirection, they call it, I believe."

"Well," I remarked, "so far everybody seems to have looked in the wrong place for our lunatic at large."

"I should be inclined, myself," said Miss Marple, "to look for somebody very sane."

"Yes," I said thoughtfully, "that's what Nash said. I remember he stressed respectability, too."

"Yes," agreed Miss Marple. "That's *very* important."

Well, we all seemed agreed.

I addressed Mrs. Calthrop. "Nash thinks," I said, "that there will be more anonymous letters. What do you think?"

"There may be," she said slowly, "I suppose."

"If the police think that, there will have to be, no doubt," said Miss Marple.

I went on doggedly to Mrs. Dane Calthrop: "Are you still sorry for the writer?"

She flushed. "Why not?"

"I don't think I agree with you, dear," said Miss Marple. "Not in this case."

I said hotly, "They've driven one woman to suicide, and caused untold misery and heartburnings!"

"Have you had one, Miss Burton?" asked Miss Marple of Joanna.

Joanna gurgled: "Oh, yes! It said the most frightful things."

"I'm afraid," said Miss Marple, "that the

people who are young and pretty are apt to be singled out by the writer.''

''That's why I certainly think it's odd that Elsie Holland hasn't had any,'' I said.

''Let me see,'' said Miss Marple. ''Is that the Symmingtons' nursery governess—the one you dreamed about, Mr. Burton?''

''Yes.''

''She's probably had one and won't say so,'' said Joanna.

''No,'' I said, ''I believe her. So does Nash.''

''Dear me,'' said Miss Marple. ''Now that's *very* interesting. That's the most interesting thing I've heard yet.''

As we were going home Joanna told me that I ought not to have repeated what Nash said about more letters coming.

''Why not?''

''Because Mrs. Dane Calthrop might be It.''

''You don't really believe that!''

''I'm not sure. She's a queer woman.''

We began our discussion of probables all over again.

It was two nights later that I was coming back in the car from Exhampton. I had had dinner there and then started back and it was already dark before I got into Lymstock.

Something was wrong with the car lights, and after slowing up and switching on and off, I finally got out to see what I could do. I was some time fiddling, but I managed to fix them up finally.

The road was quite deserted. Nobody in Lymstock is about after dark. The first few houses were just ahead, among them the ugly gabled building of the Women's Institute. It loomed up in the dim starlight and something impelled me to go and have a look at it. I don't know whether I had caught a faint glimpse of a stealthy figure flitting through the gate—if so, it must have been so indeterminate that it did not register in my conscious mind, but I did suddenly feel a kind of overweening curiosity about the place.

The gate was slightly ajar, and I pushed it open and walked in. A short path and four steps led up to the door.

I stood there a moment hesitating. What was I really doing there? I didn't know, and then, suddenly, just near at hand, I caught the sound of a rustle. It sounded like a woman's dress.

I took a sharp turn and went around the corner of the building toward where the sound had come from.

I couldn't see anybody. I went on and again turned a corner. I was at the back of the house now and suddenly I saw, only two feet away from me, an open window.

I crept up to it and listened. I could hear nothing, but somehow or other I felt convinced that there was someone inside.

My back wasn't too good for acrobatics as yet, but I managed to hoist myself up and drop over the sill inside. I made rather a noise unfortunately.

I stood just inside the window listening. Then I walked forward, my hands outstretched. I heard then the faintest sound ahead of me to my right.

I had a torch in my pocket and I switched it on.

Immediately a low, sharp voice said, "Put that out."

I obeyed instantly, for in that brief second I had recognized Superintendent Nash.

I felt him take my arm and propel me through a door and into a passage. Here, where there was no window to betray our presence to anyone outside, he switched on a lamp and looked at me more in sorrow than in anger.

"You *would* have to butt in just that minute, Mr. Burton."

"Sorry," I apologized. "But I got a hunch that I was on to something."

"And so you were probably. Did you see anyone?"

I hesitated.

"I'm not sure," I said slowly. "I've got a vague feeling I saw someone sneak in through the front gate but I didn't really see anyone. Then I heard a rustle around the side of the house."

Nash nodded. "That's right. Somebody came around the house before you. He—or she—hesitated by the window, then went on quickly—heard *you,* I expect."

I apologized again. "What's the big idea?" I asked.

Nash said:

"I'm banking on the fact that an anonymous letter writer can't stop writing letters. She may know it's dangerous, but she'll have to do it. It's like a craving for drink or drugs."

I nodded.

"Now you see, Mr. Burton, I fancy whoever it is will want to keep the letters looking the same as much as possible. She's got the cutout pages of that book, and can go on using letters and words cut out of them. But the envelopes present a difficulty. She'll want to type them on the same machine. She can't risk using another typewriter or her own handwriting."

"Do you really think she'll go on with the game?" I asked incredulously.

"Yes, I do. And I'll bet you anything you like she's full of confidence. They're always vain as hell, these people! Well, then, I figured out that whoever it was would come to the Institute after dark so as to get at the typewriter."

"Miss Ginch," I said.

"Maybe."

"You don't know yet?"

"I don't *know*."

"But you suspect?"

"Yes. But somebody's very cunning, Mr. Burton. Somebody knows all the tricks of the game."

I could imagine some of the network that Nash had spread abroad. I had no doubt that every letter written by a suspect and posted or left by hand was immediately inspected. Sooner or later the criminal would slip up, would grow careless.

For the third time I apologized for my zealous and unwanted presence.

"Oh, well," said Nash philosophically, "it can't be helped. Better luck next time."

I went out into the night. A dim figure was standing beside my car. To my astonishment I recognized Megan.

"Hullo!" she said. "I thought this was your car. What have you been doing?"

"What are you doing is much more to the point?" I said.

"I'm out for a walk. I like walking at night. Nobody stops you and says silly things, and I like the stars, and things smell better, and everyday things look all mysterious."

"All of that I grant you freely," I said. "But

only cats and witches walk in the dark. They'll wonder about you at home."

"No, they won't. They never wonder where I am or what *I'm* doing."

"How are you getting on?" I asked.

"All right, I suppose."

"Miss Holland look after you and all that?"

"Elsie's all right. She can't help being a perfect fool."

"Unkind—but probably true," I said. "Hop in and I'll drive you home."

It was not quite true that Megan was never missed.

Symmington was standing on the doorstep as we drove up.

He peered toward us.

"Hullo, is Megan there?"

"Yes," I said. "I've brought her home."

Symmington said sharply, "You musn't go off like this without telling us, Megan. Miss Holland has been quite worried about you."

Megan muttered something and went past him into the house.

Symmington sighed. "A grown-up girl is a great responsibility with no mother to look after her. She's too old for school, I suppose."

He looked toward me rather suspiciously.

"I suppose you took her for a drive?" I thought it best to leave it like that.

7

On the following day I went mad. Looking back on it, that is really the only explanation I can find.

I was due for my monthly visit to Marcus Kent. . . . I went up by train. To my intense surprise Joanna elected to stay behind. As a rule she was eager to come and we usually stayed up for a couple of days.

This time, however, I proposed to return the same day by the evening train, but even so I was astonished at Joanna. She merely said enigmatically that she'd got plenty to do, and why spend hours in a nasty stuffy train when it was a lovely day in the country?

That, of course, was undeniable, but sounded very unlike Joanna.

She said she didn't want the car, so I was to drive it to the station and leave it parked there against my return.

The station of Lymstock is situated, for some obscure reason known to railway companies only, quite half a mile from Lymstock itself. Halfway along the road I overtook Megan shuffling along in an aimless manner. I pulled up.

"Hullo, what are you doing?"

"Just out for a walk."

"But not what is called a good brisk walk, I gather. You were crawling along like a dispirited crab."

"Well, I wasn't going anywhere particular."

"Then you'd better come and see me off at the station." I opened the door of the car and Megan jumped in.

"Where are you going?" she asked.

"London. To see my doctor."

"Your back's not worse, is it?"

"No, it's practically all right again. I'm expecting him to be very pleased about it."

Megan nodded.

We drew up at the station. I parked the car and went in and bought my ticket at the booking office. There were very few people on the platform and nobody I knew.

"You wouldn't like to lend me a penny, would you?" said Megan. "Then I'd get a bit of chocolate out of the slot machine."

"Here you are, baby," I said, handing her the coin in question. "Sure you wouldn't like some clear gums or some throat pastilles as well?"

"I like chocolate best," said Megan without suspecting sarcasm.

She went off to the chocolate machine, and I looked after her with a feeling of mounting irritation.

She was wearing trodden-over shoes, and coarse unattractive stockings and a particularly shapeless jumper and skirt. I don't know why all this should have infuriated me, but it did.

I said angrily as she came back, "Why do you wear those disgusting stockings?"

Megan looked down at them, surprised. "What's the matter with them?"

"Everything's the matter with them. They're loathsome. And why wear a pullover like a decayed cabbage?"

"It's all right, isn't it? I've had it for years."

"So I should imagine. And why do you—"

At this minute the train came in and interrupted my angry lecture.

I got into an empty first-class carriage, let down the window and leaned out to continue the conversation.

Megan stood below me, her face upturned. She asked me why I was so cross.

"I'm not cross," I said untruly. "It just infuriates me to see you so slack, and not caring how you look."

"I couldn't look nice, anyway, so what does it matter?"

"Cut it!" I said. "I'd like to see you turned out properly. I'd like to take you to London and outfit you from tip to toe."

"I wish you could," said Megan.

The train began to move. I looked down into Megan's upturned, wistful face.

And then as I have said, madness came upon me.

I opened the door, grabbed Megan with one arm and fairly hauled her into the carriage.

There was an outraged shout from a porter, but all he could do was dexterously to bang shut the door again. I pulled Megan up from the floor where my impetuous action had landed her.

"What on earth did you do that for?" she demanded, rubbing one knee.

"Shut up," I said. "You're coming to London with me and when I've done with you you won't know yourself. I'll show you what you can look like if you try. I'm tired of seeing you mouch about down at heel and all anyhow."

"Oh!" said Megan in an ecstatic whisper.

The ticket collector came along and I bought Megan a return ticket. She sat in her corner looking at me in a kind of awed respect.

"I say," she said when the man had gone. "You are sudden, aren't you?"

"Very," I said. "It runs in our family."

How explain to Megan the impulse that had come over me?—She had looked like a wistful dog being left behind. She now had on her face the incredulous pleasure of the dog who has been taken on the walk after all.

"I suppose you don't know London very well?" I said to Megan.

"Yes, I do," said Megan. "I always went through it to school. And I've been to the dentist there and to a pantomime."

"This," I said darkly, "will be a different London."

We arrived with half an hour to spare before my appointment in Harley Street.

I took a taxi and we drove straight to Mirotin, Joanna's dressmaker. Mirotin is, in the flesh, an unconventional and breezy woman of forty-five, Mary Grey. She is a clever woman and very good company. I have always liked her.

I said to Megan, "You're my cousin."

"Why?"

"Don't argue," I said.

Mary Grey was being firm with a stout woman who was enamored of a skin-tight powder-blue evening dress. I detached her and took her aside.

"Listen," I said. "I've brought a little cousin of mine along. Joanna was coming up but was prevented. But she said I could leave it all to you. You see what the girl looks like now?"

"I most certainly do!" said Mary Grey with feeling.

"Well, I want her turned out right in every particular from head to foot. Carte blanche. Stockings, shoes, undies, everything! By the way, the man who does Joanna's hair is close around here, isn't he?"

"Antoine? Around the corner. I'll see to that too."

"You're a woman in a thousand."

"Oh, I shall enjoy it—apart from the money—and that's not to be sneezed at in these days—half my damned brutes of women never pay their bills. But as I say, I shall enjoy it." She shot a quick professional glance at Megan standing a little way off. "She's got a lovely figure."

"You must have X-ray eyes," I said. "She looks completely shapeless to me."

Mary Grey laughed.

"It's these schools," she said. "They seem to take a pride in turning out girls who preen themselves on looking like nothing on earth. They call it being sweet and unsophisticated. Sometimes it takes a whole season before a girl can pull herself together and look human. Don't worry, leave it all to me."

"Right," I said. "I'll come back and fetch her about six."

• • •

Marcus Kent was pleased with me. He told me that I surpassed his wildest expectations.

"You must have the constitution of an elephant," he said, "to make a comeback like this. Oh, well, wonderful what country air and no late hours or excitement will do for a man if he can only stick it."

"I grant you your first two," I said. "But don't think that the country is free from excitement. We've had a good deal in my part."

"What sort of excitement?"

"Murder," I said.

Marcus Kent pursed up his mouth and whistled. "Some bucolic love tragedy? Farm lad kills his lass?"

"Not at all. A crafty, determined lunatic killer."

"I haven't read anything about it? When did they lay him by the heels?"

"They haven't, and it's a she!"

"Whew! I'm not sure that Lymstock's quite the right place for you, old boy."

I said firmly, "Yes, it is. And you're not going to get me out of it."

Marcus Kent has a low mind. He said at once, "So that's it! Found a blonde?"

"Not at all," I said, with a guilty thought of Elsie Holland. "It's merely that the psychology of crime interests me a good deal."

"Oh, all right. It certainly hasn't done you any harm so far, but just make sure that your lunatic killer doesn't obliterate *you*."

"No fear of that," I said.

"What about dining with me this evening? You can tell me all about your revolting murder."

"Sorry. I'm booked."

"Date with a lady—eh? Yes, you're definitely on the mend."

"I suppose you could call it that," I said, rather tickled at the idea of Megan in the role.

I was at Mirotin's at six o'clock when the establishment was officially closing. Mary Grey came to meet me at the top of the stairs outside the showroom. She had a finger to her lips.

"You're going to have a shock! If I say it myself, I've put in a good bit of work."

I went on into the big showroom. Megan was standing looking at herself in a long mirror. I give you my word I hardly recognized her! For the minute it took my breath away. Tall and slim as a willow with delicate ankles and feet shown off by sheer silk stockings and well-cut shoes. Yes, lovely feet and hands, small bones—quality and distinction in every line of her. Her hair had been trimmed and shaped to her head and it was glowing like a glossy chestnut. They'd had the sense to leave her face alone. She was not made up, or if she was it was so slight and delicate that it did not show. Her mouth needed no lipstick.

Moreover there was about her something that I had never seen before, a new innocent pride in the arch of her neck. She looked at me gravely with a small, shy smile.

"I do look—rather nice, don't I?" said Megan.

"Nice?" I said. "Nice isn't the word! Come on out to dinner and if every second man doesn't turn around to look at you I'll be surprised. You'll knock all the other girls into a cocked hat."

Megan was not beautiful, but she was unusual and striking-looking. She had personality. She walked into the restaurant ahead of me and as the head waiter hurried toward us, I felt the thrill of idiotic pride that a man feels when he has got something out of the ordinary with him.

We had cocktails first and lingered over them. Then we dined. And later we danced. Megan was keen to dance and I didn't want to disappoint her, but for some reason or other I hadn't thought she would dance well. But she did. She was light as a feather in my arms, and her body and feet followed the rhythm perfectly.

"Gosh!" I said. "You can dance!"

She seemed a little surprised.

"Well, of course I can. We had dancing class every week at school."

"It takes more than dancing class to make a dancer," I said.

We went back to our table.

"Isn't this food lovely?" said Megan. "And everything!"

She heaved a delighted sigh.

"Exactly my sentiments," I said.

It was a delirious evening. I was still mad. Megan brought me down to earth when she said doubtfully, "Oughtn't we to be going home?"

My jaw dropped. Yes, definitely I was mad. I had forgotten everything! I was in a world divorced from reality, existing in it with the creature I had created.

"Good Lord!" I said.

I realized that the last train had gone.

"Stay there," I said. "I'm going to telephone."

I rang up the Llewellyn Hire people and ordered their biggest and fastest car to come around as soon as possible.

I came back to Megan.

"The last train has gone," I said. "So we're going home by car."

"Are we? What fun!"

What a nice child she was, I thought. So pleased with everything, so unquestioning, accepting all my suggestions without fuss or bother.

The car came, and it was large and fast, but all the same it was very late when we came into Lymstock.

Suddenly conscience-stricken, I said, "They'll have been sending out search parties for you!"

But Megan seemed in an equable mood. "Oh, I don't think so," she said vaguely. "I often go out and don't come home for lunch."

"Yes, my dear child, but you've been out for tea and dinner too."

However, Megan's lucky star was in the ascendant. The house was dark and silent. On Megan's advice, we went around to the back and threw stones at Rose's window.

In due course Rose looked out and with many suppressed exclamations and palpitations came down to let us in.

"Well now, and I saying you were asleep in your bed. The master and Miss Holland—" (slight sniff after Miss Holland's name) "had early supper and went for a drive. I said I'd keep an eye to the boys. I thought I heard you come in when I was up in the nursery trying to quiet Colin, who was playing up, but you weren't about when I came down so I thought you'd gone to bed. And that's what I said when the master came in and asked for you."

I cut short the conversation by remarking that that was where Megan had better go now.

"Good night," said Megan, "and thank you *awfully*. It's been the loveliest day I've ever had."

I drove home slightly lightheaded still, and tipped the chauffeur handsomely, offering him a bed if he liked. But he preferred to drive back through the night.

The hall door had opened during our colloquy and as he drove away it was flung wide open and Joanna said, "So it's you at last, is it?"

"Were you worried about me?" I asked, coming in and shutting the door.

Joanna went into the drawing room and I followed her. There was a coffee-pot on the trivet and Joanna made herself coffee while I helped myself to a whisky-and-soda.

"Worried about you? No, of course not. I thought you'd decided to stay in town and have a binge."

"I've had a binge—of a kind."

I grinned and then began to laugh.

Joanna asked what I was laughing at and I told her.

"But, Jerry, you must have been mad—quite mad!"

"I suppose I was."

"But, my dear boy, you can't do things like that —not in a place like this. It will be all around Lymstock tomorrow."

"I suppose it will. But, after all, Megan's only a child."

"She isn't. She's twenty. You can't take a girl of twenty to London and buy her clothes without a most frightful scandal. Good gracious, Jerry, you'll probably have to marry the girl."

Joanna was half serious, half laughing.

It was at that moment that I made a very important discovery.

"Damn it all," I said. "I don't mind if I do. In fact—I should like it."

A very funny expression came over Joanna's face. She got up and said drily, as she went toward the door, "Yes, I've known that for some time . . ."

She left me standing, glass in hand, aghast at my new discovery.

I don't know what the usual reactions are of a man who goes to propose marriage.

In fiction his throat is dry and his collar feels too tight and he is in a pitiable state of nervousness.

I didn't feel at all like that. Having thought of a good idea I just wanted to get it all settled as soon as possible. I didn't see any particular need for embarrassment.

I went along to the Symmingtons' house about eleven o'clock. I rang the bell and when Rose came, I asked for Miss Megan.

It was the knowing look that Rose gave me that first made me feel slightly shy.

She put me in the little morning room and while waiting there I hoped uneasily that they hadn't been upsetting Megan.

When the door opened and I wheeled around, I was instantly relieved. Megan was not looking shy or upset at all. Her head was still like a glossy chestnut, and she wore that air of pride and self-respect that she had acquired yesterday. She was in her old clothes again but she had managed to make them look different. It's wonderful what knowledge of her own attractiveness will do for a girl. Megan, I realized suddenly, had grown up.

I suppose I must really have been rather nervous, otherwise I should not have opened the conversation by saying affectionately: "Hullo, catfish!" It was hardly, in the circumstances, a loverlike greeting.

It seemed to suit Megan. She grinned and said, "Hullo!"

"Look here," I said. "You didn't get into a row about yesterday, I hope?"

Megan said with assurance, "Oh, *no*," and then blinked, and said vaguely, "Yes, I believe I did. I mean, they said a lot of things and seemed to think it had been very odd—but then you know what people are and what fusses they make all about nothing."

I was relieved to see that shocked disapproval had slipped off Megan like water off a duck's back.

"I came around this morning," I said, "because I've a suggestion to make. You see I like you a lot, and I think you like me—"

"Frightfully," said Megan with rather disquieting enthusiasm.

"And we get on awfully well together, so I think it would be a good idea if we got married."

"Oh," said Megan.

She looked surprised. Just that. Not startled. Not shocked. Just mildly surprised.

"You mean you really want to marry me?" she asked with the air of one getting a thing perfectly clear.

"More than anything in the world," I said— and I meant it.

"You mean, you're in love with me?"

"I'm in love with you."

Her eyes were steady and grave. She said, "I think you're the nicest person in the world—but I'm not in love with you."

"I'll make you love me."

"That wouldn't do. I don't want to be *made*." She paused and then said gravely, "I'm not the sort of wife for you. I'm better at hating than at loving."

She said it with a queer intensity.

I said, "Hate doesn't last. Love does."

"Is that true?"

"It's what I believe."

Again there was a silence. Then I said, "So it's 'no,' is it?"

"Yes, it's 'No.' "

"And you don't encourage me to hope?"

"What would be the good of that?"

"None whatever," I agreed. "Quite redundant in fact—because I'm going to hope whether you tell me to or not."

Well, that was that.

I walked away from the house feeling slightly dazed but irritatingly conscious of Rose's passionately interested gaze following me.

Rose had had a good deal to say before I could escape.

That she'd never felt the same since that awful day! That she wouldn't have stayed except for the children and being sorry for poor Mr. Symmington. That she wasn't going to stay unless they got another maid quick—and they wouldn't be likely to do that when there had been a murder in the house! That it was all very well for that Miss Holland to say she'd do the housework in the meantime.

Very sweet and obliging she was—oh, yes, but it was mistress of the house that she was fancying herself going to be one fine day! Mr. Symmington, poor man, never saw anything—but one knew what a widower was, a poor helpless creature made to be the prey of a designing woman. And that it wouldn't be for want of trying if Miss Holland didn't step into the dead mistress's shoes!

I assented mechanically to everything, yearning to get away and unable to do so because Rose was holding firmly on to my hat while she indulged in her flood of spite.

I wondered if there was any truth in what she said. Had Elsie Holland envisaged the possibility of becoming the second Mrs. Symmington? Or was she just a decent kindhearted girl doing her best to look after a bereaved household?

The result would quite likely be the same in either case. And why not? Symmington's young children needed a mother—Elsie was a decent soul —besides being quite indecently beautiful—a point which a man might appreciate—even such a stuffed fish as Symmington!

I thought all this, I know, because I was trying to put off thinking about Megan.

You may say that I had gone to ask Megan to marry me in an absurdly complacent frame of mind and that I deserved what I got—but it was not really like that. It was because I felt so assured, so certain, that Megan belonged to me— that she was my business, that to look after her and make her happy and keep her from harm was the only natural right way of life for me, that I had expected her to feel, too—that she and I—belonged to each other.

But I was not giving up. Oh, no! Megan was my woman and I was going to have her.

After a moment's thought, I went to Symmington's office. Megan might pay no attention to strictures on her conduct, but I would like to get things straight.

Mr. Symmington was disengaged, I was told, and I was shown into the room.

By a pinching of the lips, and an additional stiffness of manner, I gathered that I was not exactly popular at the moment.

"Good morning," I said. "I'm afraid this isn't a professional call, but a personal one. I'll put it plainly. I dare say you'll have realized that I'm in love with Megan. I've asked her to marry me and she has refused. But I'm not taking that as final."

I saw Symmington's expression change, and I read his mind with ludicrous ease. Megan was a disharmonious element in his house. He was, I felt sure, a just and kindly man, and he would never have dreamed of not providing a home for his dead wife's daughter. But her marriage to me would certainly be a relief. The frozen halibut thawed. He gave me a pale, cautious smile.

"Frankly, do you know, Burton, I had no idea of such a thing. I know you've taken a lot of notice of her, but we've always regarded her as such a child."

"She's not a child," I said shortly.

"No, no, not in years."

"She can be her age any time she's allowed to be," I said, still slightly angry. "She's not of age, I know, but she will be in a month or two. I'll let you have all the information about myself you want. I'm well off and have led quite a decent life. I'll look after her and do all I can to make her happy.''

"Quite—quite. Still, it's up to Megan herself.''

"She'll come round in time,'' I said. "But I just thought I'd like to get straight with you about it.''

He said he appreciated that, and we parted amicably.

I ran into Miss Emily Barton outside. She had a shopping basket on her arm.

"Good morning, Mr. Burton, I hear you went to London yesterday.''

Yes, she had heard all right. Her eyes were, I thought, kindly, but full of curiosity, too.

"I went to see my doctor,'' I said.

Miss Emily smiled.

That smile made little of Marcus Kent. She murmured, "I hear Megan nearly missed the train. She jumped in when it was going.''

"Helped by me,'' I said. "I hauled her in.''

"How very lucky you were there. Otherwise there might have been an accident.''

It is extraordinary how much of a fool one gentle, inquisitive, old maiden lady can make a man feel!

I was saved further suffering by the onslaught of Mrs. Dane Calthrop. She had her own tame elderly maiden lady in tow, but she herself was full of direct speech.

"Good morning,'' she said. "I hear you've made Megan buy herself some decent clothes? Very sensible of you. It takes a man to think of something really practical like that. I've been worried about that girl for a long time. Girls with brains are so liable to turn into morons, aren't they?"

With which remarkable statement, she shot into the fish shop.

Miss Marple, left standing by me, twinkled a little and said, "Mrs. Dane Calthrop is a very remarkable woman, you know. She's nearly always right."

"It makes her rather alarming," I said.

"Sincerity has that effect," said Miss Marple.

Mrs. Dane Calthrop shot out of the fish shop again and rejoined us. She was holding a large red lobster.

"Have you ever seen anything so unlike Mr. Pye?" she said. "Very virile and handsome, isn't it?"

I was a little nervous of meeting Joanna but I found when I got home that I needn't have worried. She was out and she did not return for lunch. This aggrieved Partridge a good deal, who said sourly as she proffered two loin chops in an entrée dish:

"Miss Burton said specially as she was going to be *in*."

I ate both chops in an attempt to atone for Joanna's lapse. All the same, I wondered where my sister was. She had taken to being very mysterious about her doings of late.

It was half past three when Joanna burst into the drawing room. I had heard a car stop outside and I half expected to see Griffith, but the car drove on and Joanna came in alone.

Her face was very red and she seemed upset. I perceived that something had happened.

"What's the matter?" I asked.

Joanna opened her mouth, closed it again, sighed, plumped herself down in a chair and stared in front of her.

She said, "I've had the most awful day."

"What's happened?"

"I've done the most incredible things. It was awful—"

"But what—"

"I just started out for a walk, an ordinary walk—I went up over the hill and on to the moor. I walked miles—I felt like it. Then I dropped down into a hollow. There's a farm there—a God-forsaken lonely sort of spot. I was thirsty and I wondered if they had any milk or something. So I wandered into the farmyard and then the door opened and Owen came out."

"Yes?"

"He thought it might be the district nurse. There was a woman in there having a baby. He was expecting the nurse and he'd sent word to her to get hold of another doctor. It—things were going wrong."

"Yes?"

"So he said—to *me*. 'Come on, you'll do—better than nobody.' I said I couldn't, and he said what did I mean? I said I'd never done anything like that, that I didn't know anything—

"He asked me what the hell that mattered. And then he was *awful*. He turned on me. He said, 'You're a woman, aren't you? I suppose you can do your durnedest to help another woman?' And he went on at me—said I'd talked as though I was interested in doctoring and had said I wished I was a nurse. 'All pretty talk, I suppose! You didn't mean anything real by it, but this *is* real and you're going to behave like a decent human being and not a useless ornamental nitwit!'

"I've done the most indiscernible things, Jerry. Held instruments and boiled them and handed things. I'm so tired I can hardly stand up. It was dreadful. But he saved her—and the baby. It was born alive. He didn't think at one time he could save it. Oh, dear!"

Joanna covered her face with her hands.

I contemplated her with a certain amount of pleasure and mentally took my hat off to Owen Griffith. He'd brought Joanna slap up against reality for once.

I said, "There's a letter for you in the hall. From Paul, I think."

"Eh?" She paused for a minute and then said, "I'd no idea, Jerry, what doctors had to do. The nerve they've got to have!"

I went out into the hall and brought Joanna her letter. She opened it, glanced vaguely at its contents, and let it drop.

"He was—really—rather wonderful. The way he fought—the way he wouldn't be beaten! He was rude and horrible to *me*—but he *was* wonderful."

I observed Paul's disregarded letter with some pleasure. Plainly, Joanna was cured of Paul.

Things never come when they are expected.

I was full of Joanna's and my personal affairs and was quite taken aback the next morning when Nash's voice said over the telephone:

"*We've got her,* Mr. Burton!"

I was so startled I nearly dropped the receiver.

"You mean the—"

He interrupted: "Can you be overheard where you are?"

"No, I don't think so—well, perhaps—"

It seemed to me that the baize door to the kitchen had swung open a trifle.

"Perhaps you'd care to come down to the station?"

"I will. Right away."

I was at the police station in next to no time. In an inner room Nash and Sergeant Parkins were together. Nash was wreathed in smiles.

"It's been a long chase," he said. "But we're there at last."

He flicked a letter across the table. This time it was all typewritten. It was, of its kind, fairly mild:

It's no use thinking you're going to step into a dead woman's shoes. The whole town is laughing at you. Get out now. Soon it will be too late. This is a warning. Remember what happened to that other girl. Get out and stay out.

It finished with some mildly obscene language.

"That reached Miss Holland this morning," said Nash.

"Thought it was funny she hadn't had one before," said Sergeant Parkins.

"Who wrote it?" I asked.

Some of the exultation faded out of Nash's face.

He looked tired and concerned. He said soberly:

"I'm sorry about it, because it will hit a decent man hard, but there it is. Perhaps he's had his suspicions already."

"Who wrote it?" I reiterated.

"Miss Aimée Griffith."

• • •

Nash and Parkins went to the Griffiths' house that afternoon with a warrant.

By Nash's invitation I went with them.

"The doctor," he said, "is very fond of you. He hasn't many friends in this place. I think if it is not too painful to you, Mr. Burton, that you might help him to bear up under the shock."

I said I would come. I didn't relish the job, but I thought I might be some good.

We rang the bell and asked for Miss Griffith and we were shown into the drawing room. Elsie Holland, Megan and Symmington were there having tea.

Nash behaved very circumspectly.

He asked Aimée if he might have a few words with her privately.

She got up and came toward us. I thought I saw just a faint hunted look in her eye. If so, it went again. She was perfectly normal and hearty.

"Want me? Not in trouble over my car lights again, I hope?"

She led the way out of the drawing room and across the hall into a small study.

As I closed the drawing-room door, I saw Symmington's head jerk up sharply. I supposed his legal training had brought him in contact with police cases, and he had recognized something in Nash's manner. He half rose.

That is all I saw before I shut the door and followed the others.

Nash was saying his piece. He was very quiet and correct. He cautioned her and then told her that he must ask her to accompany him. He had a warrant for her arrest and he read out the charge.

I forget now the exact legal term. It was the letters, not murder yet.

Aimée Griffith flung up her head and bayed with laughter. She boomed out:

"What ridiculous nonsense! As though I'd write a packet of indecent stuff like that. You must be mad. I've never written a word of the kind."

Nash had produced the letter to Elsie Holland. He said, "Do you deny having written this, Miss Griffith?"

If she hesitated it was only for a split second.

"Of course I do. I've never seen it before."

Nash said quietly:

"I must tell you, Miss Griffith, that you were observed to type that letter on the machine at the Women's Institute between eleven and eleven-thirty P.M. on the night before last. Yesterday you entered the post office with a bunch of letters in your hand—"

"I never posted this."

"No, you did not. While waiting for stamps, you dropped it inconspicuously on the floor, so that somebody should come along unsuspectingly and pick it up and post it."

"I never—"

The door opened and Symmington came in. He said sharply, "What's going on? Aimée, if there is anything wrong, you ought to be legally represented. If you wish me—"

She broke then. Covered her face with her hands and staggered to a chair. She said, "Go away, Dick, go away. Not you! Not *you*!"

"You need a solicitor, my dear girl."

"Not you. I—I couldn't bear it. I don't want you to know—all this."

He understood then, perhaps. He said quietly, "I'll get hold of Mildmay, of Exhampton. Will that do?"

She nodded. She was sobbing now.

Symmington went out of the room. In the doorway he collided with Owen Griffith.

"What's this?" said Owen violently. "My sister—"

"I'm sorry, Dr. Griffith. Very sorry. But we have no alternative."

"You think she—was responsible for those letters?"

"I'm afraid there is no doubt of it, sir," said Nash—he turned to Aimée: "You must come with us now, please, Miss Griffith—you shall have every facility for seeing a solicitor, you know."

Owen cried, "Aimée?"

She brushed past him without looking at him.

She said, "Don't talk to me. Don't say anything. And for heaven's sake don't *look* at me!"

They went out. Owen stood like a man in a dream.

I waited a bit, then I came up to him.

"If there's anything I can do, Griffith, tell me."

He said like a man in a dream, "Aimée? I don't believe it."

"It may be a mistake," I suggested feebly.

He said slowly, "She wouldn't take it like that if it were. But I would never have believed it. I *can't* believe it."

He sank down on a chair. I made myself useful by finding a stiff drink and bringing it to him. He swallowed it down and it seemed to do him good.

He said, "I couldn't take it in at first. I'm all right now. Thanks, Burton, but there's nothing you can do. Nothing *anyone* can do."

The door opened and Joanna came in. She was very white.

She came over to Owen and looked at me.

She said, "Get out, Jerry. This is my business."

As I went out of the door, I saw her kneel down by his chair.

8

I can't tell you coherently the events of the next twenty-four hours. Various incidents stand out, unrelated to other incidents.

I remember Joanna coming home, very white and drawn and of how I tried to cheer her up, saying:

"Now who's being a ministering angel?"

And of how she smiled in a pitiful twisted way and said, "He says he won't have me, Jerry. He's very *very* proud and stiff!"

And I said, "My girl won't have me either. . . ."

We sat there for a while, Joanna saying at last, "The Burton family isn't exactly in demand at the moment!"

I said, "Never mind, my sweet, we still have each other," and Joanna said, "Somehow or other, Jerry, that doesn't comfort me much just now. . . ."

Owen came the next day and rhapsodized in the

most fulsome way about Joanna. She was wonderful, marvelous! The way she'd come to him, the way she was willing to marry him—at once if he liked. But he wasn't going to let her do that. No, she was too good, too fine to be associated with the kind of muck that would start as soon as the papers got hold of the news.

I was fond of Joanna, and knew she was the kind who's all right when standing by in trouble, but I got rather bored with all this highfalutin stuff. I told Owen rather irritably not to be so damned noble.

I went down to the High Street and found everybody's tongue wagging nineteen to the dozen. Emily Barton was saying that she had never really trusted Aimée Griffith. The grocer's wife was saying with gusto that she'd always thought Miss Griffith had a queer look in her eye—

They had completed the case against Aimée, so I learned from Nash. A search of the house had brought to light the cut pages of Emily Barton's book—in the cupboard under the stairs, of all places, wrapped up in an old roll of wallpaper.

"And a jolly good place too," said Nash appreciatively. "You never know when a prying servant won't tamper with a desk or a locked drawer—but those junk cupboards full of last year's tennis balls and old wallpaper are never opened except to shove something more in."

"The lady would seem to have had a penchant for that particular hiding place," I said.

"Yes. The criminal mind seldom has much variety. By the way, talking of the dead girl, we've got one fact to go upon: There's a large heavy pestle missing from the doctor's dispensary. I'll bet anything you like that's what she was stunned with."

"Rather an awkward thing to carry about," I objected.

"Not for Miss Griffith. She was going to the Guides that afternoon, but she was going to leave flowers and vegetables at the Red Cross stall on the way, so she'd got a whopping great basket with her."

"You haven't found the skewer?"

"No, and I shan't. The poor devil may be mad, but she wasn't mad enough to keep a bloodstained skewer just to make it easy for us, when all she'd got to do was to wash it and return it to a kitchen drawer."

"I suppose," I conceded, "that you can't have everything."

The vicarage had been one of the last places to hear the news. Old Miss Marple was very much distressed by it. She spoke to me very earnestly on the subject:

"It isn't *true*, Mr. Burton. I'm sure it isn't true."

"It's true enough, I'm afraid. They were lying in wait, you know. They actually *saw* her type that letter."

"Yes, yes—perhaps they did. Yes, I can understand *that*."

"And the printed pages from which the letters were cut were found where she'd hidden them in her house."

Miss Marple stared at me. Then she said, in a very low voice, "But that is horrible—really *wicked*."

Mrs. Dane Calthrop came up with a rush and

joined us and said, "What's the matter, Jane?"

Miss Marple was murmuring helplessly, "Oh, dear, oh, dear, what can one *do*?"

"What's upset you, Jane?"

Miss Marple said, "There must be *something*. But I am so old and so ignorant and, I am afraid, so foolish."

I felt rather embarrassed and was glad when Mrs. Dane Calthrop took her friend away.

I was to see Miss Marple again that afternoon, however. Much later when I was on my way home.

She was standing near the little bridge at the end of the village, near Mrs. Cleat's cottage, and talking to Megan, of all people.

I wanted to see Megan. I had been wanting to see her all day. I quickened my pace. But as I came up to them, Megan turned on her heel and went off in the other direction.

It made me angry and I would have followed her, but Miss Marple blocked my way.

"I wanted to speak to you," she said. "No, don't go after Megan now. It wouldn't be wise."

I was just going to make a sharp rejoinder when she disarmed me by saying, "That girl has great courage—a very high order of courage."

I still wanted to go after Megan, but Miss Marple said, "Don't try and see her now. I do know what I am talking about. She must keep her courage intact."

There was something about the old lady's assertion that chilled me. It was as though she knew something that I didn't.

I was afraid and didn't know why I was afraid.

I didn't go home. I went back into the High Street and walked up and down aimlessly. I don't know what I was waiting for, nor what I was thinking about. . . .

I got caught by that awful old bore Colonel Appleby. He asked after my pretty sister as usual and then went on:

"What's all this about Griffith's sister being mad as a hatter? They say she's been at the bottom of this anonymous letter business that's been such a confounded nuisance to everybody? Couldn't believe it at first, but they say it's quite true."

I said it was true enough.

"Well, well—I must say our police force is pretty good on the whole. Give 'em time, that's all, give 'em time. Funny business this anonymous letter stunt—these desiccated old women are always the ones who go in for it—though the Griffith woman wasn't bad-looking even if she was a bit long in the tooth. But there aren't any decent-looking girls in this part of the world— except that governess girl of the Symmingtons. She's worth looking at. Pleasant girl, too. Grateful if one does any little thing for her.

"Came across her having a picnic or something with those kids not long ago. They were romping about in the heather and she was knitting—ever so vexed she'd run out of wool. 'Well,' I said, 'like me to run into Lymstock? I've got to call for a rod of mine there. I shan't be more than ten minutes getting it, then I'll run you back again.' She was a bit doubtful about leaving the boys. 'They'll be all right,' I said. 'Who's to harm them?' Wasn't going to have the boys along, no fear! So I ran her in, dropped her at the wool shop, picked her up again later and that was that. Thanked me very prettily. Grateful and all that. Nice girl."

I managed to get away from him.

It was after that, that I caught sight of Miss Marple for the third time. She was coming out of the police station.

Where do one's fears come from? Where do they shape themselves? Where do they hide before coming out into the open?

Just one short phrase. Heard and noted and never quite put aside:

"Take me away— It's so awful being here— feeling so wicked . . ."

Why had Megan said that? What had she to feel wicked about?

There could be nothing in Mrs. Symmington's death to make Megan feel wicked.

Why had the child felt wicked? Why? Why?

Could it be because she felt responsible in any way?

Megan? Impossible! *Megan* couldn't have had anything to do with those letters—those foul obscene letters.

Owen Griffith had known a case up north—a schoolgirl . . .

What had Inspector Graves said?

Something about an *adolescent mind* . . .

Innocent middle-aged ladies on operating tables babbled words they hardly knew. Little boys chalking up things on walls.

No, no, not *Megan.*

Heredity? Bad blood? An unconscious inheritance of something abnormal? Her misfortune, not her fault, a curse laid upon her by a past generation?

"I'm not the wife for you. I'm better at hating than loving."

Oh, my Megan, my little child. Not *that*! Anything but that. And that old Tabby is after you, she suspects. She says you have courage. Courage to do *what*?

It was only a brainstorm. It passed. But I wanted to see Megan—I wanted to see her badly.

At half past nine that night I left the house and went down to the town and along to the Symmingtons'.

It was then that an entirely new idea came into my mind. The idea of a woman whom nobody had considered for a moment.

(Or had Nash considered her?)

Wildly unlikely, wildly improbable, and I would have said up to today impossible, too. But that was not so. No, not *impossible*.

I redoubled my pace. Because it was now even more imperative that I should see Megan straightaway.

I passed through the Symmingtons' gate and up to the house. It was a dark overcast night. A little rain was beginning to fall. The visibility was bad.

I saw a line of light from one of the windows. The little morning room?

I hesitated a moment or two, then instead of going up to the front door, I swerved and crept very quietly up to the window, skirting a big bush and keeping low.

The light came from a chink in the curtains, which were not quite drawn. It was easy to look through and see.

It was a strangely peaceful and domestic scene. Symmington in a big armchair, and Elsie Holland, her head bent, busily patching a boy's torn shirt.

I could hear as well as see, for the window was open at the top.

Elsie Holland was speaking:

"But I do think, really, Mr. Symmington, that the boys are quite old enough to go to boarding school. Not that I shan't hate leaving them because I shall. I'm ever so fond of them both."

Symmington said, "I think perhaps you're right about Brian, Miss Holland. I've decided that he shall start next term at Winhays—my old prep school. But Colin is a little young yet. I'd prefer him to wait another year."

"Well, of course I see what you mean. And Colin is perhaps a little young for his age—"

Quiet domestic talk—quiet domestic scene—and a golden head bent over needlework.

Then the door opened and Megan came in.

She stood very straight in the doorway, and I was aware at once of something tense and strung up about her. The skin of her face was tight and drawn and her eyes bright and resolute. There was no diffidence about her tonight and no childishness.

She said, addressing Symmington, but giving him no title (and I suddenly reflected that I never had heard her call him anything. Did she address him as father or as Dick or what?):

"I would like to speak to you, please. Alone."

Symmington looked surprised and, I fancied, not best pleased. He frowned, but Megan carried her point with a determination unusual in her.

She turned to Elsie Holland and said, "Do you mind, Elsie?"

"Oh, of course." Elsie Holland jumped up. She looked startled and a little flurried.

She went to the door and Megan came farther in so that Elsie passed her.

Just for a minute Elsie stood motionless in the doorway looking over her shoulder.

Her lips were closed, she stood quite still, one hand stretched out, the other clasping her needlework to her.

I caught my breath, overwhelmed suddenly by her beauty.

When I think of her now, I always think of her like that—in arrested motion, with that matchless deathless perfection that belonged to ancient Greece.

Then she went out shutting the door.

Symmington said rather fretfully, "Well, Megan, what is it? What do you want?"

Megan had come right up to the table. She stood there looking down at Symmington. I was struck anew by the resolute determination of her face and by something else—a hardness new to me.

Then she opened her lips and said something that startled me to the core.

"I want some money," she said.

The request didn't improve Symmington's temper. He said sharply, "Couldn't you have waited until tomorrow morning? What's the matter, do you think your allowance is inadequate?"

A fair man, I thought even then, open to reason, though not to emotional appeal.

Megan said, "I want a good deal of money."

Symmington sat up straight in his chair. He said coldly:

"You will come of age in a few months' time. Then the money left you by your grandmother will be turned over to you by the Public Trustee."

Megan said:

"You don't understand. I want money from *you*." She went on, speaking faster: "Nobody's ever talked much to me about my father. They've not wanted me to know about him. But I do know that he went to prison and I know why. It was for blackmail!"

She paused.

"Well, I'm his daughter. And perhaps I take after him. Anyway, I'm asking you to give me money because—if you don't—" She stopped and then went on very slowly and evenly—"if you don't—*I shall say what I saw you doing to the cachet that day in my mother's room.*"

There was a pause. Then Symmington said in a completely emotionless voice, "I don't know what you mean."

Megan said, "I think you do."

And she smiled. It was not a nice smile.

Symmington got up. He went over to the writing desk. He took a checkbook from his pocket and wrote out a check. He blotted it carefully and then came back. He held it out to Megan.

"You're grown up now," he said. "I can understand that you may feel you want to buy something rather special in the way of clothes and all that. I don't know what you're talking about. I didn't pay attention. But here's a check."

Megan looked at it, then she said, "Thank you. That will do to go on with."

She turned and went out of the room. Symmington stared after her and at the closed door, then he turned around and as I saw his face I made a quick uncontrolled movement forward.

It was checked in the most extraordinary fashion. The big bush that I had noticed by the wall stopped being a bush. Superintendent Nash's arms went around me and Superintendent Nash's voice just breathed in my ear:

"Quiet, Burton. For God's sake."

Then, with infinite caution he beat a retreat, his arm impelling me to accompany him.

Around the side of the house he straightened himself and wiped his forehead.

"Of course," he said. "You *would* have to butt in!"

"That girl isn't safe," I said urgently. "You saw his face? We've got to get her out of here."

Nash took a firm grip of my arm.

"Now, look here, Mr. Burton, you've got to *listen*."

Well, I listened.

I didn't like it—but I gave in.

But I insisted on being on the spot and I swore to obey orders implicitly.

So that is how I came with Nash and Parkins into the house by the back door, which was already unlocked.

And I waited with Nash on the upstairs landing behind the velvet curtain masking the window alcove until the clocks in the house struck two, and Symmington's door opened and he went across the landing and into Megan's room.

I did not stir or make a move for I knew that Sergeant Parkins was inside masked by the opening door, and I knew that Parkins was a good man and knew his job, and I knew that I couldn't have trusted myself to keep quiet and not break out.

And waiting there, with my heart thudding, I saw Symmington come out with Megan in his arms and carry her downstairs, with Nash and myself a discreet distance behind him.

He carried her through to the kitchen and he had just arranged her comfortably with her head in the gas oven and had turned on the gas when Nash and I came through the kitchen door and switched on the light.

And that was the end of Richard Symmington. He collapsed. Even while I was hauling Megan out and turning off the gas I saw the collapse. He didn't even try to fight. He knew he'd played and lost.

Upstairs I sat by Megan's bed waiting for her to come around and occasionally cursing Nash.

"How do you know she's all right? It was too big a risk."

Nash was very soothing.

"Just a soporific in the milk she always had by her bed. Nothing more. It stands to reason, he couldn't risk her being poisoned. As far as he's concerned the whole business is closed with Miss Griffith's arrest. He can't afford to have any mysterious death. No violence, no poison. But if a rather unhappy type of girl broods over her mother's suicide, and finally goes and puts her head in the gas oven—well, people just say that she was never quite normal and the shock of her mother's death finished her."

I said, watching Megan, "She's a long time coming around."

"You heard what Dr. Griffith said? Heart and pulse quite all right—she'll just sleep and wake naturally. Stuff he gives a lot of his patients, he says."

Megan stirred. She murmured something.

Superintendent Nash unobtrusively left the room.

Presently Megan opened her eyes.

"Jerry."

"Hullo, sweet."

"Did I do it well?"

"You might have been blackmailing ever since your cradle!"

Megan closed her eyes again. Then she murmured:

"Last night—I was writing to you—in case anything went—went wrong. But I was too sleepy to finish. It's over there."

I went across to the writing table. In a shabby little blotter I found Megan's unfinished letter.

"My dear Jerry," it began primly:

"I was reading my school Shakespeare and the sonnet that begins:

> " 'So are you to my thoughts as food to life
> Or as sweet-season'd showers are to the
>   ground'

and I see that I am in love with you after all, because that is what I feel." . . .

"So you see," said Mrs. Dane Calthrop, "I was quite right to call in an expert."

I stared at her. We were all at the vicarage. The rain was pouring down outside and there was a pleasant log fire, and Mrs. Dane Calthrop had just wandered around, beat up a sofa cushion and put it for some reason of her own on the top of the grand piano.

"But did you?" I said, surprised. "Who was it? What did he do?"

"It wasn't a he," said Mrs. Dane Calthrop.

With a sweeping gesture she indicated Miss Marple. Miss Marple had finished the fleecy knitting and was now engaged with a crochet hook and a ball of cotton.

"That's my expert," said Mrs. Dane Calthrop. "Jane Marple. Look at her well. I tell you, that woman knows more about the different kinds of human wickedness than anyone I've ever known."

"I don't think you should put it quite like that, dear," murmured Miss Marple.

"But you do."

"One sees a good deal of human nature living in a village all the year around," said Miss Marple placidly.

Then, seeming to feel it was expected of her, she laid down her crochet, and delivered a gentle old-maidish dissertation on murder.

"The great thing in these cases is to keep an absolutely open mind. Most crimes, you see, are so absurdly simple. This one was. Quite sane and straightforward—and quite understandable—in an unpleasant way, of course."

"Very unpleasant!"

"The truth was really so very obvious. You saw it, you know, Mr. Burton."

"Indeed I did not."

"But you did. You indicated the whole thing to me. You saw perfectly the relationship of one thing to the other, but you just hadn't enough self-confidence to see what those feelings of yours meant. To begin with, that tiresome phrase 'No smoke without fire.' It irritated you, but you proceeded quite correctly to label it for what it was—a smoke screen. Misdirection, you see—everybody looking at the wrong thing—the anonymous letters, but the whole point was that there *weren't* any anonymous letters!''

''But, my dear Miss Marple, I can assure you that there *were*. I had one.''

''Oh, yes, but they weren't real at all. Dear Maud here tumbled to that. Even in peaceful Lymstock there are plenty of scandals, and I can assure you any *woman* living in the place would have known about them and used them. But a man, you see, isn't interested in gossip in the same way—especially a detached logical man like Mr. Symmington. But a genuine woman writer of those letters would have made her letters much more to the point.

''So you see that if you disregard the smoke and come to the fire you know where you are. You just come down to the actual facts of what happened. And putting aside the letters, just one thing happened—Mrs. Symmington died.

''So then, naturally, one thinks of who might have wanted Mrs. Symmington to die, and of course the very first person one thinks of in such a case is, I am afraid, the *husband*. And one asks oneself is there any *reason?*—any *motive?*—for instance, *any other woman?*

''And the very first thing I hear is that there is a very attractive young governess in the house. So clear, isn't it? Mr. Symmington, a rather dry repressed unemotional man, tied to a querulous and neurotic wife and then suddenly this radiant young creature comes along.

''I'm afraid, you know, that gentlemen, when

they fall in love at a certain age, get the disease very badly. It's quite a madness. And Mr. Symmington, as far as I can make out, was never actually a *good* man—he wasn't very kind or very affectionate or very sympathetic—his qualities were all negative—so he hadn't really the strength to fight his madness. And in a place like this, only his wife's death would solve his problem. He wanted to marry the girl, you see. She's very respectable and so is he. And besides, he's devoted to his children and didn't want to give them up. He wanted everything, his home, his children, his respectability and Elsie. And the price he would have to pay for that was murder.

"He chose, I do think, a very clever way. He knew so well from his experience of criminal cases how soon suspicion falls on the husband if a wife dies unexpectedly—and the possibility of exhumation in the case of poison. So he created a death which seemed only incidental to something else. He created a nonexistent anonymous letter writer. And the clever thing was that the police were certain to suspect a *woman*—and they were quite right in a way. All the letters were a woman's letters; he cribbed them very cleverly from the letters in the case last year and from a case Dr. Griffith told him about. I don't mean that he was so crude as to reproduce any letter verbatim, but he took phrases and expressions from them and mixed them up, and the net result was that the letters definitely represented a woman's mind—a half-crazy repressed personality.

"He knew all the tricks that the police use, handwriting, typewriting tests, etc. He's been preparing his crime for some time. He typed all the envelopes before he gave away the typewriter to the Women's Institute, and he cut the pages from the book at Little Furze probably quite a long time ago when he was waiting in the drawing room one day. People don't open books of sermons much!

"And finally, having got his false Poison Pen well established, he staged the real thing. A fine afternoon when the governess and the boys and his stepdaughter would be out, and the servants having their regular day out. He couldn't foresee that the little maid Agnes would quarrel with her ·boy friend and come back to the house."

Joanna asked, "But what did she see? Do you know that?"

"I don't *know*. I can only guess. My guess would be that she didn't see anything."

"That it was all a mare's nest?"

"No, no, my dear, I mean that she stood at the pantry window all the afternoon waiting for the young man to come and make it up and that— quite literally she saw nothing. That is, *no one* came to the house at all, not the postman, nor anybody else.

"It would take her some time, being slow, to realize that that was very odd—because apparently Mrs. Symmington *had* received an anonymous letter that afternoon."

"Didn't she receive one?" I asked, puzzled.

"But of course not! As I say, this crime is so simple. Her husband just put the cyanide in the top cachet of the ones she took in the afternoon when her sciatica came on after lunch. All Symmington had to do was to get home before, or at the same time as Elsie Holland, call his wife, get no answer, go up to her room, drop a spot of cyanide in the plain glass of water she had used to swallow the cachet, toss the crumpled-up anonymous letter into the grate, and put by her hand the scrap of paper with '*I can't go on*' written on it.''

Miss Marple turned to me.

"You were quite right about that, too, Mr. Burton. A 'scrap of paper' was all wrong. People don't leave suicide notes on small torn scraps of paper. They use a *sheet* of paper—and very often an envelope too. Yes, the scrap of paper was wrong and you knew it.''

"You are rating me too high," I said. "I knew nothing."

"But you did, you really *did*, Mr. Burton. Otherwise why were you immediately impressed by the message your sister left scribbled on the telephone pad?''

I repeated slowly: " 'Say that *I can't go on Friday*'—I see! '*I can't go on*'?''

Miss Marple beamed on me.

"Exactly. Mr. Symmington came across such a message and saw its possibilities. He tore off the words he wanted for when the time came—a message genuinely in his wife's handwriting.''

"Was there any further brilliance on my part?" I asked.

Miss Marple twinkled at me.

"You put me on the track, you know. You assembled those facts together for me—in sequence—and on top of it you told me the most important thing of all—that Elsie Holland had never received any anonymous letters.''

"Do you know," I said, "last night I thought that *she* was the letter writer and that that was why there had been no letters written to her?''

"Oh, dear me, no. . . . The person who writes anonymous letters practically always sends them to herself as well. That's part of the—well, the excitement, I suppose. No, no, the fact interested me for *quite* another reason. It was really, you see, Mr. Symmington's one weakness. He couldn't bring himself to write a foul letter to the girl he loved. It's a very interesting sidelight on human nature—and a credit to him, in a way—but it's where he gave himself away."

Joanna said, "And he killed Agnes? But surely that was quite unnecessary?"

"Perhaps it was, but what you don't realize, my dear (not having killed anyone), is that your judgment is distorted afterward and everything seems exaggerated. No doubt he heard the girl telephoning to Partridge, saying she'd been worried ever since Mrs. Symmington's death, that there was something she didn't understand. He can't take any chances—this stupid foolish girl has seen *something*, knows something."

"Yet apparently he was at his office all that afternoon?"

"I should imagine he killed her before he went. Miss Holland was in the dining room and kitchen. He just went out into the hall, opened and shut the front door as though he was going out, then slipped into the little cloakroom.

"When only Agnes was left in the house, he probably rang the front-door bell, slipped back into the cloakroom, came out behind her and hit her on the head as she was opening the front door, and then after thrusting the body into the cupboard, he hurried along to his office, arriving just a little late if anyone had happened to notice it, but they probably didn't. You see, no one was suspecting a *man*."

"Abominable brute," said Mrs. Dane Calthrop.

"You're not sorry for him, Mrs. Dane Calthrop?" I inquired.

"Not in the least. Why?"

"I'm glad to hear it, that's all."

Joanna said:

"But why Aimée Griffith? I know that the police have found the pestle taken from Owen's dispensary—and the skewer too. I suppose it's not so easy for a man to return things to kitchen drawers. And guess where they were? Superintendent Nash only told me just now when I met him on my way here. In one of those musty old deed boxes in his office. Estate of Sir Jasper Harrington-West, deceased."

"Poor Jasper," said Mrs. Dane Calthrop. "He was a cousin of mine. Such a correct old boy. He would have had a fit!"

"Wasn't it madness to keep them?" I asked.

"Probably madder to throw them away," said Mrs. Dane Calthrop. "No one had any suspicions about Symmington."

"He didn't strike her with the pestle," said Joanna. "There was a clock weight there too, with hair and blood on it. He pinched the pestle, they think, on the day Aimée was arrested, and hid the book pages in her house. And that brings me back to my original question. What about Aimée Griffith? The police actually *saw* her write that letter."

"Yes, of course," said Miss Marple. "She did write *that* letter."

"But why?"

"Oh, my dear, surely you have realized that Miss Griffith had been in love with Symmington all her life?"

"Poor thing!" said Mrs. Dane Calthrop mechanically.

"They'd always been good friends, and I daresay she thought, after Mrs. Symmington's death, that some day, perhaps—well—" Miss Marple coughed delicately. "And then the gossip began spreading about Elsie Holland and I expect that upset her badly. She thought of the girl as a designing minx worming her way into Symmington's affections and quite unworthy of him. And so, I think, she succumbed to temptation. Why not add one more anonymous letter, and frighten the girl out of the place? It must have seemed quite safe to her and she took, as she thought, every precaution."

"Well?" said Joanna. "Finish the story."

"I should imagine," said Miss Marple slowly, "that when Miss Holland showed that letter to Symmington he realized at once who had written it, and he saw a chance to finish the case once and for all, and make himself safe. Not very nice—no, not very nice, but he was frightened, you see. The police wouldn't be satisfied until they'd got the anonymous letter writer. When he took the letter down to the police and he found they'd actually seen Aimée writing it, he felt he'd got a chance in a thousand of finishing the whole thing.

"He took the family to tea there that afternoon and as he came from the office with his attaché case, he could easily bring the torn-out book pages to hide under the stairs and clinch the case. Hiding them under the stairs was a neat touch. It recalled the disposal of Agnes' body, and, from the practical point of view, it was very easy for him. When he followed Aimée and the police, just a minute or two in the hall passing through would be enough.''

"All the same," I said, "there's one thing I can't forgive you for, Miss Marple—roping in Megan."

Miss Marple put down her crochet which she had resumed. She looked at me over her spectacles and her eyes were stern.

"My dear young man, *something* had to be done. There was no evidence against this very clever and unscrupulous man. I needed someone to help me, someone of high courage and good brains. I found the person I needed."

"It was very dangerous for her."

"Yes, it was dangerous, but we are not put into this world, Mr. Burton, to avoid danger when an innocent fellow creature's life is at stake. You understand me?"

I understood.

It was morning in the High Street.

Miss Emily Barton came out of the grocer's with her shopping bag. Her cheeks were pink and her eyes were excited.

"Oh, dear, Mr. Burton, I really am in such a flutter. To think I really am going on a cruise at last!"

"I hope you'll enjoy it."

"Oh, I'm sure I shall. I should never have dared to go by myself. It does seem so *providential* the way everything has turned out. For a long time I've felt that I ought to part with Little Furze, that my means were really too straitened, but I couldn't bear the idea of *strangers* there.

"But now that you have bought it and are going to live there with Megan—it is quite different. And then dear Aimée, after her terrible ordeal, not quite knowing what to do with herself, and her brother getting married (how nice to think you have *both* settled down with us!), and agreeing to come with me. We mean to be away quite a long time. We might even"—Miss Emily dropped her voice—"*go around the world!* And Aimée is so splendid and so practical. I really do think—don't you?—that everything turns out for the *best*."

Just for a fleeting moment I thought of Mrs. Symmington and Agnes Woddell in their graves in the churchyard and wondered if they would agree, and then I remembered that Agnes' boy friend hadn't been very fond of her and that Mrs. Symmington hadn't been very nice to Megan and, what the hell? We've all got to die some time! And I agreed with happy Miss Emily that everything was for the best in the best of possible worlds.

I went along the High Street and in at the Symmingtons' gate and Megan came out to meet me.

It was not a romantic meeting because an outsize old English sheep dog came out with Megan and nearly knocked me over with his ill-timed exuberance.

"Isn't he *adorable*?" said Megan.

"A little overwhelming. Is he ours?"

"Yes, he's a wedding present from Joanna. We *have* had nice wedding presents, haven't we? That fluffy woolly thing that we don't know what it's for from Miss Marple, and the lovely Crown Derby tea set from Mr. Pye, and Elsie has sent me a toast rack—"

"How typical!" I interjected.

"And she's got a post with a dentist and is very happy. And—where was I?"

"Enumerating wedding presents. Don't forget if you change your mind you'll have to send them all back."

"I shan't change my mind. What else have we got? Oh, yes, Mrs. Dane Calthrop has sent an Egyptian scarab."

"Original woman," I said.

"Oh! Oh! But you don't know the best. *Partridge* has actually sent me a present. It's the most hideous tea cloth you've ever seen. But I think she *must* like me now because she says she embroidered it all with her own hands."

"In a design of sour grapes and thistles, I suppose?"

"No; true lover's knots."

"Dear, dear," I said, "Partridge *is* coming on."

Megan had dragged me into the house.

She said:

"There's just one thing I can't make out. Besides the dog's own collar and lead, Joanna has sent an extra collar and lead. What do you think that's for?"

"That," I said, "is Joanna's little joke."

AGATHA CHRISTIE

Mystery's #1 Bestseller!

"One of the most imaginative and fertile plot creators of all time!"
—Ellery Queen

Agatha Christie is the world's most brilliant and most famous mystery writer, as well as one of the greatest storytellers of all time. And now, Berkley presents a mystery lover's paradise—35 classics from this unsurpassed Queen of Mystery.

"Agatha Christie...what more could a mystery addict desire?"
—The New York Times

Available Now

___06778-5 **CARDS ON THE TABLE**
___06797-1 **THE PATRIOTIC MURDERS**
___06791-2 **MURDER IN MESOPOTAMIA**
___06793-9 **MURDER IN THREE ACTS**
___06803-X **THERE IS A TIDE...**
___06777-7 **THE BOOMERANG CLUE**
___06804-8 **THEY CAME TO BAGHDAD**
___06788-2 **MR. PARKER PYNE, DETECTIVE**
___06795-5 **THE MYSTERIOUS MR. QUIN**
___06781-5 **DOUBLE SIN AND OTHER STORIES**
___06808-0 **THE UNDER DOG AND OTHER STORIES**

___06787-4 **THE MOVING FINGER**
___06801-3 **SAD CYPRESS**
___06799-8 **POIROT LOSES A CLIENT**
___06776-9 **THE BIG FOUR**
___06780-7 **DEATH IN THE AIR**
___06784-X **THE HOLLOW**
___06796-3 **N OR M?**
___06802-1 **THE SECRET OF CHIMNEYS**
___06800-5 **THE REGATTA MYSTERY AND OTHER STORIES**
___06798-X **PARTNERS IN CRIME**
___06806-4 **THREE BLIND MICE AND OTHER STORIES**
___06785-8 **THE LABORS OF HERCULES**

All titles are $2.95
Prices may be slightly higher in Canada.

NGAIO MARSH

BESTSELLING PAPERBACKS BY A "GRAND MASTER" OF THE MYSTERY WRITERS OF AMERICA.

NGAIO MARSH

___ 07507-8	NIGHT AT THE VULCAN	$2.95
___ 06822-5	OVERTURE TO DEATH	$2.50
___ 07505-1	PHOTO FINISH	$2.95
___ 07504-3	WHEN IN ROME	$2.95
___ 06014-3	COLOUR SCHEME	$2.50
___ 07440-3	DEAD WATER	$2.95
___ 06700-8	DEATH AT THE BAR	$2.50
___ 06007-0	FALSE SCENT	$2.50
___ 05967-6	THE NURSING HOME MURDER	$2.50
___ 06179-4	SPINSTERS IN JEOPARDY	$2.50
___ 06015-1	TIED UP IN TINSEL	$2.50
___ 06012-7	VINTAGE MURDER	$2.50
___ 06016-X	A WREATH FOR RIVERA	$2.50
___ 06497-1	SCALES OF JUSTICE	$2.50

Prices may be slightly higher in Canada.

Available at your local bookstore or return this form to:

 JOVE
Book Mailing Service
P.O. Box 690, Rockville Centre, NY 11571

Please send me the titles checked above. I enclose _____. Include 75¢ for postage and handling if one book is ordered; 25¢ per book for two or more not to exceed $1.75. California, Illinois, New York and Tennessee residents please add sales tax.

NAME_____

ADDRESS_____

CITY _____ STATE/ZIP_____

(allow six weeks for delivery.)   SK-7/b